AUTHOR Niall. Ian.	CLASS No. C F.
TITLE The village policeman.	BOOK No. 97120976

D1351467

The Village Policeman

The Village Policeman

IAN NIALL

HEINEMANN : LONDON

William Heinemann Ltd
15 Queen St, Mayfair, London W1X 8BE
LONDON MELBOURNE TORONTO
JOHANNESBURG AUCKLAND

First published 1971
© Ian Niall 1971

434 51017 3

Printed in Great Britain by
Western Printing Services Ltd, Bristol

Contents

Dedicated to the late P.C. Arthur Howell Williams and his faithful companion and wife, Mary Ellen, who lived for a good part of their lives at the County Police Station in Abergynolwyn, Merioneth.

For the Record

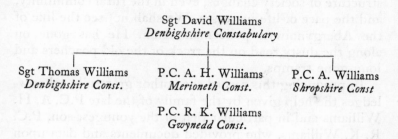

Sgt David Williams
Denbighshire Constabulary

Sgt Thomas Williams
Denbighshire Const.

P.C. A. H. Williams
Merioneth Const.

P.C. A. Williams
Shropshire Const

P.C. R. K. Williams
Gwynedd Const.

The Constabularies of Denbigh and Merioneth are now defunct, both having been incorporated, along with the Constabulary of Anglesey and Caernarvon, into the Gwynedd Constabulary, which takes its name from the ancient Welsh kingdom.

Sergeant David Williams was the father of three policemen and the grandfather of one. When he himself came to the end of his service he was the recipient of an illuminated address from the people of Llansilin in Denbighshire, who also presented him with a 'purse of money' as a token of the esteem in which they held him. This kind of gesture cannot be made today. Regulations forbid the police authority accepting a fund to benefit an individual policeman on his retirement. The village policeman can never be quite the man he once was and the public is the poorer for that. A time was when a boy robbing an orchard took his punishment on the spot and didn't appear before the bench, indeed had he done so

the magistrates might have looked askance at the policeman concerned. Today society gives the juvenile offender
a record from the outset and the country policeman is
involved in this whether he likes it or not. He is no longer
an arbiter, no longer the village headman, and unlikely
to stand in the community alongside the rector and the
squire, or carry the collection up the aisle on Sunday. The
structure of society changes, even in the rural community,
and the pace of life increases. We shall not see the like of
the Abergynolwyn policeman again. He has gone on
along the dusty road on the track of the old poachers and
long-gone tramps.

    In producing this record the author gratefully acknow-
ledges the help given by the family of the late P.C. A. H.
Williams and in particular that of the youngest son, P.C.
R. K. Williams, who provided documents and data upon
which much of the book is based.

I

Clean Nose, Taffy!

LETTER HOME:

'The beat at night is like a nightmare. One morning, after my first time out I saw a goldfinch in a cage in a dirty shop. There should be a law against trapping goldfinches when they end up in such a place as this.'

HIS introduction to the beat was made by the old sergeant who waited for him on the steps of the station, his hands tucked up into the sleeves of the greatcoat which fitted tightly on his portly figure and made him seem shorter than he really was. Police Constable Arthur Howell Williams was tall and lean. His greatcoat didn't fit as well as the sergeant's. He hadn't discovered the tailor who, for a shilling or so, made a policeman's uniform fit in places where it had formerly sagged. There was apparently only one sort of policeman, a standard-shaped one. The cut uniform took no account of long-limbed, lean fellows from the Welsh hills, any more than it allowed for sergeants with rotund bellies.

'One thing, Taffy,' said the sergeant as they walked in step along the long wet street. 'One thing, whatever else you do, keep a clean nose! A clean nose is the first concern of a good policeman.'

P.C. 11 nodded his head and almost collided with the sergeant when his superior suddenly stooped and looked about the pavement:

'Damn it!' he said. 'I've dropped it!'

Without asking what it was the sergeant had dropped, P.C. Williams began at once to help him look for it. 'It' wasn't to be found, however, and the sergeant cursed again until his companion saw something in the gutter and picked it up.

'Is this what you dropped, Sergeant?' he asked.

The object he had found was a fat little short-stemmed pipe with a silver cap. The sergeant took it eagerly.

'Damn it again,' he said. 'It is full of water!'

The pipe, P.C. Williams decided, was a special one, designed to slip up the sergeant's sleeve if the inspector came on the scene, a neat, fat pipe for a neat fat man, but it was full of the black water of a Manchester gutter. The sergeant wouldn't be able to enjoy a smoke until it was clean and dried out.

'Another thing,' said the sergeant. 'Discretion, see? A constable sees all sorts of things. He learns when to keep his mouth shut. He takes note and learns.'

In the gloom of the overhanging warehouse wall P.C. Williams allowed himself to smile. Policemen were very much alike in Manchester and Wales, where his father served in the Denbighshire Constabulary. A clean nose and use discretion. His father had said exactly that.

'You won't find much warmth in them,' he had told him. 'They're not the same people, see? But you keep your nose clean, whatever happens. Accept no favours and you don't have to give any! Learn to keep your mouth shut. See all but say little. Put it down in the little book in your mind. Remember it. You become a good police-man by living and experiencing things—and remembering.'

Good old Dad, straight as a die. No pipe up his sleeve,

for he wasn't one to indulge in tobacco or drink. Now here he was, P.C. 11, newly-recruited into the Manchester City Police, following in father's footsteps and nineteen years of age.

'Now them boots o' yours will probably hurt your feet,' said the sergeant as he pushed the pipe down into his pocket. 'You want to look after your feet. This job is endless walk, lad, up one side of the street, down the other, up the next street, on and on. All you got between you and the road is your boots.'

'My boots are broken in, Sergeant,' he said. 'I wore them on the postman's round, see?'

Boots were a part of a policeman's dress that authority expected him to buy for himself. P.C. Williams had been well advised. He had come to Manchester in well-worn boots. Indeed, he had had hardly enough money to buy new ones had he wanted to.

'You've had good advice, lad,' said the sergeant.

'My Dad's in the police,' he said.

'That's right, Eleven, I forgot. Your Dad give you some advice. Mark you lad, this is Manchester. There's no hills, and no sheep but black ones here! There's everything here you won't see in Wales, from thieves to tarts.'

Once again the young constable couldn't help smiling. Hills and sheep maybe, but thieves and tarts! A Manchester sergeant hadn't much idea about Wales. There were thieves and tarts there in fair proportion. His father had hauled many a one into the front room to be charged with picking pockets or being drunk and riotous. People were the same everywhere. But Manchester seemed to have a monopoly of tannery smells, fog, and grime.

'You check the time carefully,' advised the sergeant, 'and make sure you're not late at the meeting place. You pull every padlock and try the door latch. You walk this side one night and that side the next. Sometimes you go half way up one side and cross over and go half way up the other, doing it the opposite way round on the road back, see? You listen and report anything suspicious, anything at all, and you be careful if somebody asks you to step up an entry to a drunk man or a sick woman. Keep your truncheon so that you can pull it. Think to get your back to the wall if you're threatened. If you can't get your truncheon out remember your helmet is just as good for belting them with!'

They plodded on. What the sergeant had to say endorsed the instruction the recruit had already received, but now he was about to be launched on the beat. The world seemed darker and the figures that peopled it more furtive and sinister. Men huddled close to walls, lights in warehouses seemed dimmer. The street lamps had their own halo of yellow mist about them. Manchester streets were not like the streets of his native place. The first public house they came to brooded at the junction of two cavernous rows of warehouses in a place where no one lived or walked the pavement.

'So now we come to the Spinner's Arms,' said the sergeant, 'and I show you something that you put down under discretion, see?'

The sergeant didn't go in through the door that bore the frosted legend Public Bar, but turned into the yard at the side. P.C. Williams flashed his lantern from one stack of beer barrels to another. The sergeant walked over to a dimly-lit window and knocked quietly on it with his wool-gloved knuckles. A moment or two later the window opened.

'Anybody in?'

'Only Jack Hackett.'

The sergeant reached forward and accepted the pint pot that was placed on the window-sill.

'Nobody else.'

'This is a new constable, P.C. Williams, a Taffy,' said the sergeant. 'I'm showing him the beat.'

'Will he have one?'

'He won't,' said the sergeant. 'He's either teetotal or a Welsh Baptist. They're both against it.'

P.C. Williams felt himself being scrutinized by a man whose face was in shadow.

'Takes all sorts,' said the publican.

The sergeant wiped his moustache and put the pint pot on the window-sill once more. The window closed. The two policemen turned and went back out on to the street.

'Si'thee lad,' said the sergeant, 'don't do as I do, do as I say. I don't know whether you're a Baptist or not. I don't much care. The pints on this beat are for your sergeant. Don't think because he's supped some himself he can't tell if you've been at it! Keep your nose clean, lad, and you'll get on. This is where you learn discretion.'

They went on up the road, P.C. Williams fondling a hundred padlocks and putting his shoulder to doors and gates, the sergeant stopping at the Rose and Crown, the Black Lion, the Carpenter's Arms and two or three more where tankards awaited him at the back door.

'A man who sups ale regularly gets used to the stuff,' said the sergeant. 'It doesn't dim his faculties the same.'

P.C. Williams had to admire the sergeant's capacity but he was sick of the smell of pub yards and reeking, slippery-floored urinals.

'Well lad,' said the sergeant as they turned at the end of their long walk. 'We've seen the place. We've met who should have met us. We're on our way home. We won't walk the way we came. We won't call in for any more ale. Never do anything to a pattern, see? The bad lads are watching you wherever you go. Tomorrow somebody'll be in saying one of them warehouses has been burgled while the watchman was asleep. Where were you at eleven o'clock! In the yard of the Queen's supping ale?'

There was nothing the young constable could say. It was hard to understand these foreigners.

'Where I call I ask who's in,' said the sergeant. 'They tell me. They know I can easily pop in the bar and check up. Next day if something is reported I know who was about and who wasn't. I get an idea who was missing, or who was near to. I know who to go knocking up . . .'

Off duty, P.C. Williams went back up the stairs of the section house feeling depressed. Manchester in the dark was so much bigger than Manchester in daylight. Walking the beat by night was like exploring a rat colony, a series of endless tunnels with nothing well-enough lit. He sat on his bed and took off his boots, letting them thud on to the floor as he did so. His heart was heavy. Pangs of *hiraeth* came upon him and he knew the awful homesickness of the Welsh-*hiraeth* to be back in the village, to be with the family, in familiar places.

'What's up, Taff?' asked the man lying on the adjoining bed.

'I feel a bit sick,' he confessed.

The other constable scratched himself and turned over:

'Too much beer, maybe. It's stronger than your Welsh stuff! You want to remember that. You take all they offer you and you'll slosh so the sergeant can hear you. Won't need to smell your breath!'

'I was with the sergeant,' he said wearily.

'Then you never got so much as a drop! I forgot you was out for the first time. Tomorrow, though, you can sup a drop and maybe you won't be so miserable.'

P.C. Williams got into bed after saying his prayers. In a minute he was asleep, dreaming about the sunlit slopes of the mountain where he trapped goldfinches as a boy. The minister was in his dream, catching him on a Sunday with a caged nicol, as they called goldfinches in that part of Wales. 'Aren't you afraid that you might catch the

hairy hand of the devil, doing such a thing on a Sunday?'
asked the minister and he grinned and said, 'I'd catch
anything, sir, if it would sing for me!' It was half a dream,
and half a recollection of something that had happened.
As a dream it was sweet. The sky was blue, the goldfinches tinkling on their way across the thistle field in a
world blessed by the warmth of the sun.

The world to which he awoke in the morning was the
grim Manchester one. The only birds he heard were
sparrows that fluttered down to pick between the feet of
the horses as they waited to haul their loads and their
drivers ate their morning snack. The gaslamps were out.
If a man peered intently he could see a church spire or a
tall building rising out of the mist. The music of the
morning wasn't the singing of the bird. It was the hollow
booming of a vessel coming up the canal or the strident
note of a tramcar's bell as the lurching and rattling con-
veyance trundled to the city, making street litter dance
in the wind of its back-draught.

'No goldfinch would stop here,' he found himself
saying as he went into the street. 'If it did it wouldn't
sing.'

A little way along one of the grimy streets, however, he
did see a goldfinch, a rather sooty, miserable bird with a
bald head, for it had not long been imprisoned and had
worn away its head feathers rushing at the top of the cage.

'Five shillings,' said the man in the shop.

His would-be customer sighed. If he had had five
shillings the goldfinch might have gone free. The thought
of its imprisonment made him full of remorse to think he
had ever trapped them.

'Sign the book then,' ordered the sergeant when he presented himself for duty that evening.

'It should be made illegal to trap goldfinches, Sergeant,'
he said as he put the pencil down.

The sergeant looked at him and shrugged his shoulders. 'You concern yourself with what is illegal already, lad! You got enough there to worry about without asking for more laws. On your way now, and don't miss any doors or we might have you on the carpet tomorrow!'

He was on his own now, following the lamplighter who swayed and bobbed along the streets, reaching up to flip open the door of the lamp, applying the torch to the gas jet after the long pole had tripped the tap over, and all this without getting off his bicycle! The lamplighter seemed to be off on an equally endless journey, lighting up the grimy world from Salford to Ashton and places beyond. The lamps he left burning stood in pools of light that served to intensify the darkness in between. They made navigating points along the road, marked his progress from one stretch of doors and warehouse gates to the next, but it was a lonely road and often he found himself listening to the echo of his own footsteps ringing back from a long brick wall or down the canyon of a narrow entry between buildings. He paused, listened and tramped on. The beat was long periods of nothing, someone had laughingly remarked, sleep between lamps, a kind of black dream.

The lamplighter hadn't done his job too well, it seemed. Away up the road the pattern of light was broken. One lamp was out. As he walked on towards the long stretch of unlit pavement P.C. Williams wondered about the lamp that had been missed. Perhaps it was out of order? He came to it at last and was even more puzzled, for he could hear the hissing sound of escaping gas. The light has gone out? He flashed his lamp about and saw the broken glass and the half brick. Someone has hurled the brick at the lamp, some idle boy with nothing else to do. Was this a thing to be reported? He stood pondering for a minute, phrasing the thing as he knew it should be phrased: 'I observed broken glass and a half brick lying on the ground close to the lamp standard. The gas was escaping . . . I climbed up the lamp standard and turned it off . . .' Was this part of his duty? He decided to complete his row of doors and padlocks and think a little longer about it. Climbing dirty lamp standards wasn't the thing he objected to, but he didn't care for the ridicule of the clever Lancastrians who might tell him that this happened every day and he would be better getting a job with the gas company!

The gateway nearest to the lamp was the first he had checked that was not as it should have been. Some clerk, in a hurry to be off home had forgotten the padlock. Now he had something to report, but first he must enter and look round the yard beyond and make sure all was well. His lantern didn't give as much light as he could have wished. He saw the lumpy outlines of old, dilapidated packing cases, the railing on the stone steps leading to a doorway. Slowly he mounted the steps and checked the door. It was firmly shut. It was locked. There was no sound from within. He turned and went back down the steps and let himself out into the street again. Immediately he had done this he gently opened the gate again and tip-toed back across the yard, his lantern hidden under the skirt of his greatcoat. He found his way to the top of the steps and stood there listening for several minutes. He could hear nothing but the ticking of a clock somewhere inside, but the warehouse was as silent as a locked church. Imagination had made the hair on the back of his neck stand up. Now he laughed at himself. Going back across the yard he shone the lantern to light his way and began phrasing his report: 'I found the gate unsecured and investigated. There was no sign of anyone having effected an entry. The main door was locked. There was no pad-lock available and I was not able to secure the entrance from the street.'

It sounded well enough. He pulled out his watch and

took note of the time. The night was young but black as ever, and more lonely than night in the hills above Ffestiniog or Bala. The broken glass of the gaslamp crunched under his boots as he went on again, shouldering a gate here, turning the handle of a door there, steering his way by lamps, for there were no other landmarks visible. After he had gone perhaps a quarter of a mile he began to feel uneasy. He thought about the unfastened gate and the unlit lamp. Supposing the lamp had been put out so that whatever was to be stolen from the warehouse could be brought on to the road without being seen? He had checked the door, but supposing the thieves had seen him coming? Supposing they had lain in hiding while he checked and checked again and were now happily getting on with the job? He tried to think what might be used to carry away the stuff if not a horse and cart. A horse and cart would be conspicuous and any policeman seeing one plodding down the deserted road would wonder about it. He had seen no sign of a horse and cart, and heard nothing such as the clumping of the horse's feet or the rattle of wheels on the cobbles, and yet he worried. Perhaps the horse and cart had stood quietly in one of the entries waiting for him to pass. Once again he began to write his report: 'After considering what I had found I returned to the scene to keep observation . . .' No, that wouldn't do. 'I proceeded on my beat and met P.C. Copley and told him of my suspicions. We went to the Armatage warehouse and together kept watch.'

For at least a hundred yards the thing seemed feasible and he was almost content until he heard the squealing sound of a stiff axle and the rumble of something on the cobbles. It wasn't a cart, for there was no jingle of harness and no sound of horse's feet. He stepped into a doorway and pressed himself into the shadows as the source of the sound drew nearer. A man in a dark overcoat and cloth cap came into sight, briefly, on the far side of the road.

The man was pushing a handcart and going down the road to the warehouse! Now the report would have to be phrased differently, but P.C. Williams had no time to think about that. He knew where the handcart would stop. He knew what was going to happen.

Try not to run, his father had told him, unless the man you are after is escaping. Keep a suspect in sight all the time if you can. He tried not to run and kept the handcart just in sight, listening in case it stopped and the man pushing it heard him hurrying after him. The cart rattled and jolted on, hugging the shadows. It stopped at the Armatage warehouse and the man who had been pushing it disappeared into the yard beyond the gate, leaving the cart under the unlit lamp. The time had come to investigate and make an arrest, as it comes to every young policeman on his first night duty. P.C. Williams straightened up, drew his truncheon from his trouser pocket, set his helmet firmly on his head and went to the gate. The warehouse yard was as silent as ever, but the door at the top of the steps was open. Beyond it a dimmed light revealed the outlines of three men struggling with something they were bringing towards the door. The policeman waited, thinking of what his father had told him: 'Never give a suspect an even chance . . . work it out to your best advantage and get him when he is least able to strike back. Do it quickly, and with all the force you need to overcome him. In this job you don't get paid for your bruises or broken bones. You may get a commendation, but if you meet a Charles Peace you won't live to read it!'

The men worked their way through the doorway and began to bring the safe down the steps, grunting and panting and cursing as they did so. The policeman's hand tightened on the handle of the truncheon. He stepped forward.

'All right,' he said, 'leave it there and I'll put it back!'

They didn't leave it. They whirled about, one of them

jumping the rail down into the yard and falling heavily, one springing at him and meeting his swinging truncheon, the third dashing in through the warehouse door. Quickly P.C. Williams stooped and grabbed the man who had jumped the railing. It didn't take him a moment to get a handcuff on him. The man he had hit with his truncheon was getting to his feet but offered no resistance. He hauled the first man to the railing and forced his hand-cuffed wrist through.

'Now,' he said to the other one, 'put your hand in this.'

The second man hesitated and then, as the truncheon came up, obediently put his hand into the dangling handcuff. Now both men were linked to each other through the railing.

'You wait here,' said P.C. Williams without smiling. 'I'll be back for you.'

'Welsh bastard!' said one of them, but he didn't stop to reply.

Inside the warehouse there was no light. The lantern the thieves had carried was nowhere to be seen. His own light barely penetrated the vast area of the building. He closed the door behind him and began a search that proved quite hopeless. If there was no way out the third man had trapped himself. It would be a long wait until morning, but there was nothing else for it. In any case, when he didn't report someone would be sent out to find him, according to what the sergeant had told him. He went back out to his prisoners and stood silently at the top of the steps looking down at them.

'Well,' said one of them, 'you goin' t' keep us here all bloody night?'

'Unless your mate comes out and gives himself up,' he said.

'That's a hope! Give us a fag.'

He ignored the request and said no more. He knew that even with the third man under arrest he could hardly expect to take all three in. The situation wasn't going to change. He still must wait like a dog at a rabbit hole, trusting that there was no escape hole at the back.

It was midnight before someone came. He heard the handcart being moved about and gripped his truncheon, thinking for a moment, that some friends of the thieves had come to investigate. He took a chance and blew his whistle. A moment later the gate flapped back and the portly figure of the sergeant filled the entrance.

'You all right, Eleven?' he inquired.

'All right Sergeant,' he said with relief. 'I got two and one may be inside.'

'Welsh bastard!' repeated the man at his feet.

P.C. Williams swore back at him in Welsh, but with no vehemence and almost laughing. The sergeant came bundling up the steps, looked down at the two handcuffed men and nodded:

'You done well, lad, for a new recruit that shouldn't be on late for a month or two. I know this pair. I know who's inside, too.'

'Come out Harry!' he shouted through the warehouse door. 'You can't fool me. I know there's no back entry and you can't get up to the windows, so come out in case I come in there and bring you out. You don't want that, do you? I'm too old and too fat now to have any patience with you. Come on!'

The sergeant shone his lantern. After a minute a figure appeared in its beam. P.C. Williams stood to one side, waiting with his truncheon in his hand, but the old sergeant gave him no sign and the man who had tried to escape came out and stood sullenly looking at his captor.

'Put your hand in my pocket, lad, and bring out the bracelets.'

The thief obeyed.

'Put them on him, Eleven. You got your third one!'

The handcuffs were put on and between them the

sergeant and the young constable took their prisoners in. Their arrival created a stir among the men coming off duty.

'Taffy landed three of them!' they said, and thumped him on the shoulder. The sergeant frowned at them and jerked his head to let them know their presence was unwelcome.

'Now, Taffy,' he said, 'their statements, when they been cautioned. We got enough work to keep you out o' bed until you go back on duty again, so lick your pencil!'

It was mid-morning before he got to bed. Someone going on duty offered him a cup of tea which he sleepily refused.

In the afternoon he was summoned to the station below to be briefed for his appearance in court. He had written things in his notebook, remembering his father's advice, but no one seemed very interested in what he had written. The sergeant had been present when the third man surrendered and his report was a model of correctitude.

'Well, Taffy,' said the man on duty, 'you make sure you look right tomorrow morning, and don't get nervous if anyone asks you a question. This is an easy case. They've all been at it before. They've all been in the lock-up and served time in quod. They keep a room for them at Strangeways!'

He read his notebook over and over again, but there was no need to refresh his memory with the events of the night before. He couldn't forget it and never would.

'The gaslamp was out, sir,' he said when called to the witness box, the following day, correcting himself hastily, 'The gaslamp was out, Your Worships, and when I tried the door of the warehouse after finding the gate unpadlocked I discovered that it was locked, as it should have been, but later I thought there was some connexion between the lamp being out and the padlock being off the gate and I went back when I saw a man pushing a handcart. The handcart stopped outside Armatage's and the man went in. I followed him in and saw the three accused. I managed to apprehend two of them but the third one got away. I waited by the door until help came and on the instructions of Sergeant Potts I put the handcuffs on the third man, who gave himself up to the sergeant.'

The chairman of the Bench looked keenly at him.

'By the sound of your voice,' he said, 'I imagine you are a Welshman and new to the city. I must congratulate you on your courage and resourcefulness in apprehending these men.'

The three men looked at him and scowled. He knew what they were thinking, but it didn't worry him. He was happy and proud of himself. He would have been satisfied with it all but for the belated comment of the inspector who conducted the case.

'Williams,' he said, 'you have one weakness all you fellows from Wales seem to suffer from. You're an impulsive chap. Now next time you find anything of this sort you don't tackle it by yourself. You summon help. What has happened chalks one up for us, but it could have been the other way round. You could have been laid out and the safe could have been trundled away. Instead of getting your name in front of the Chief you'd be on the carpet for not reporting your suspicions.'

That night, when he had no duty because of his appearance in court, he sat down and wrote a letter to his father, telling him about everything that had happened, including the inspector's warning.

'They don't seem to take to us here,' he said, 'but I don't exactly take to them either! If I ever get a chance I'm going to ask to be put on a beat where there's a Welshman I can talk to sometimes. I miss the sound of Welsh.'

The letter was a long one and its writing, even although it was in his native tongue, was not accomplished without much sighing and grunting. It concerned his first case and his first arrest. Others would follow. Most of them would be less dramatic and he would be concerned with more common offences, like obstructing the footpath or spitting on the pavement.

2

A Mole in Ffestiniog

EVIDENCE IN COURT:

'Defendant used a blasphemous expression and was abusive when I arrested him. He said I didn't take her something purse. She is a something, something liar. I have written the words on a piece of paper, your worships.'

THE sergeant was pleased with him and he was going to do well, said the section-house gossip. Wait and see, they said. It would be easy for him for he had made a good start and, besides, there were one or two taffies up the tree. They were bound to look out for a fellow taffy, weren't they? He didn't tell them that he had no wish to get on. His heart shrank from the very idea of spending the rest of his time in Manchester. He didn't belong in the place and already he was thinking of going back home. The only drawback was that if he applied to join some other force it might be hard to get in when they checked up and found he hadn't stuck to the Manchester Force. He would have to give it time, but it would be like a prison sentence. The thieves that had been caught had gone to Strangeways and here he was, serving a sentence of the same kind. The only difference was the bars. Twice he had sat down to write to his father using a phrase in

Welsh that came to his mind almost every hour of the day —*gwell twrch daear yn 'Stiniog na dyn ym Manceinion* —better a mole in Ffestiniog than a man in Manchester. No one could pretend that Ffestiniog was the most beautiful place in Wales. It was a grey place, wet, shrouded in mist, made miserable by the dreary atmosphere of a slate town that supported people barely above the line of poverty, but oh, how the sun shone there when it did shine! How the buzzard sailed in the sky above the crags when the gorse was in bloom. At such times Ffestiniog was infinitely preferable to the greenest park in the Manchester suburbs. At such times even the mole emerging from the earth for a brief look at the sky was better off in Ffestiniog than he, Arthur Williams, was in Manchester!

The letters were carefully torn up and put on the fire because he knew only too well what his father would say: 'It is only the beginning of things that is hard. It is hard to be a soldier and be sent away from home. It is hard to be a policeman and not among your own people. In the cities they hate the police. You must get used to that. You must get used to the place and the job you do. Stick at it, son. Nobody ever won by running away.' He didn't need to send the letters when he knew what the reply would be but he had a hankering to write directly to the Chief Constable of Merioneth and ask him if there might be a place for him on the County Force. 'I am a Welshman, sir,' he found himself saying, 'and I find it hard here. I was responsible for the arrest of three men not long ago and got a commendation for it but I don't want to live here and if you would take me I would be glad to serve in any village you might send me to.' This letter, however, remained unwritten and he nursed his depression and homesickness day after day, early and late, until something happened that quite put the thought from his mind.

He was on duty on a Saturday afternoon when he recognized a pickpocket whose description had been circulated only a day or two before. The man was hurrying to join people going into a church hall outside which a noticeboard carried a bill telling the world that a bazaar was in progress. It seemed a reasonable hunting ground for a pickpocket and the tall young Welsh constable made haste to follow him through the door. The charge for admission was only a penny but the gentleman taking the money smiled and let him through as he peered beyond him at the disappearing figure of the suspect.

Always try to be as inconspicuous as you can, his father had told him, and try to look casual when you are on the heels of a suspect. Don't give him an excuse for making a dash for it or you may find that people get in your way and he escapes. It wasn't easy to be inconspicuous and more than six feet in height with a helmet on top, but he did his best until, in his eagerness to get close to the man he was after, he blundered into a trestle table and almost brought it to the ground. Everyone seemed to look round. He bent down and pulled the trestle leg back under its load and at the same time slipped his helmet off and let it dangle from his hand by the chinstrap. They had rules about this, too, of course. A constable was improperly dressed in a public place without his helmet on his head, and this was a public place, but the pickpocket might have seen the helmet and would be looking for it above the heads of the crowd. There were times when rules and regulations took no account of what a man might have to do. He gently shouldered his way through a group of women who were turning over secondhand dresses and apologized when one of them frowned at him.

'Should be out on the street, not dodging it in here,' she said to her companion, 'but that's the police for you.'

He knew all about that, too. The police were lazy. They

were dishonest and cunning. The public were the industrious ones and they were always honest! Serve the silly woman right if the pickpocket already had her purse!

The pickpocket had evidently run into some kind of bother in the far corner of the hall for there was a sudden outburst of voices and a milling of people from whose midst the man finally emerged, ploughing and butting his way along regardless of those in his way. P.C. Williams reached down from above and caught him by the collar. The little man thrashed and struggled like a newly-gaffed salmon but he couldn't get away and at last he was brought in or hauled from between two startled ladies to come to a standstill at the policeman's side.

'All right,' he said. 'Where you going in such a hurry then?'

The pickpocket kicked out and the tall policeman's eyes watered with the pain he suffered.

'I've got a cure for that,' said the angry Welshman bringing out his truncheon. 'Do it again and you'll be charged with more than picking pockets. You'll get a taste of this as well, see, boy?'

The sight of the truncheon seemed to quell the little man's enthusiasm for violence. P.C. Williams was putting his truncheon away again when his captive suddenly twisted free and dived into the crowd once more.

'Shut that door, if you please!' called the policeman. The door of the hall was firmly closed.

There was only one thing for it now, he told himself. He must join the doorkeeper and wait until the man gave himself up or until everyone else had left the hall. No point in sending for assistance when there was no other way out and a search was impracticable. He went to the door and explained.

'We've got a well-known pickpocket in here,' he said. 'I followed him in. Now I can't search the place with this crowd here but so long as that door at the top stays barred he can't get out. So if you don't mind I'll just wait here for him and he'll fall into my hands in the end.'

The man on the door regarded him soberly for a moment and then grinned.

'I could get you taking the money maybe?' he suggested. 'After all, since we're open until nine tonight you could pass the time doing a bit of good for the church?'

Nine o'clock and he was off at five! There was no help for it, however. He stood at the door and kept his eye on the people filing in and out. The pickpocket knew what he was about and didn't venture near the door. Once again it was a sort of rabbit-hole vigil. He had no ferret to put down after his quarry.

'Would you like to buy something?' asked the young woman on the stall nearest to the door.

He looked at her. She was well-rounded, pretty, dark-haired and about his own age.

'Well,' he said, flushing, 'I'm on duty, see? I'm waiting here to catch a pickpocket. That's what I came in for.'

She smiled at him and he almost forgot what he had come in for! Mechanically he dug his hand in his pocket and brought out the few coppers he had in his possession.

'Here,' he said. 'I'm a church man myself.'

'Not a Welsh Baptist?' she asked.

Everyone seemed to have heard of Welsh Baptists and no one seemed to know that there was a church in Wales.

'Not a Baptist,' he said.

'What's your name?'

'Arthur Williams,' he said, 'Arthur Howell Williams from Llansilin in Denbighshire where my father is a policeman.'

She thought about this for a minute. 'My name is Mary Ellen Stafford and I live in Accrington,' she said. 'My friend and I are dressmakers. We work together and we offered to help with the bazaar. I've taken twenty-three shillings already.'

'And fourpence,' he said.

She smiled, and reaching out pinned an artificial flower on to his uniform. His embarrassment was acute. The regulations were quite explicit about decorations. He was not allowed to wear anything in his buttonhole or to pin anything on his uniform except with the permission of the authority, and that only a medal won in the service of H.R.H. or her late Royal Highness Queen Victoria. He looked down at the flower and didn't know what to do about it, for her hand lingered and she was smiling up at him, turning his head with every second that passed.

'I'm not supposed to—' he said and then he suddenly saw the pickpocket slipping past. 'No!' he groaned, rushing through the door and dropping his helmet which rolled round and round on the pavement until he rushed back and grabbed it. The pickpocket was away like a hare, dodging through between a cart and a brewer's dray and diving up a narrow entry, his coat tails flapping like the wings of a frantic hen. P.C. Williams pulled out his whistle and began to blow it for all he was worth even although he needed his breath to keep running. The labyrinth of streets and alleys seemed to swallow the escaping man and the shrilling of the police whistle echoed back from all sides. Defeated, P.C. Williams came to a halt and put the whistle away. Now he had to report the incident. Now he had to go back and see if there was someone who could identify the pickpocket and someone who had a complaint.

The man on the door looked inquiringly at him.

'He beat me,' he confessed. 'I ran as hard as I could but he knows the entries better than I do.'

'Well that's a pity because he's got this lady's purse and her friend saw him take it.'

The complaint was going to be made and he saw himself up before the sergeant. 'How did he manage to slip past you, Eleven?' he heard the sergeant say. 'I was talking to a young woman, Sergeant . . .' It was something that was going to wipe out his commendation all right, and all the sympathy the young woman might lavish upon him would do no good.

'I'll keep a watch out for him,' said Mary Ellen Stafford. 'I wish he hadn't got away but you'll see him again. I'm sure of that!'

He wasn't at all sure, but her smile lifted his spirits as he turned to take a statement from the lady who had lost her purse.

'It's all right lad,' she said. 'I only had a sixpence in it and the purse was an old one.'

He hesitated a moment. 'I'm sorry, missis,' he said, 'but it's the same as if you'd had a sovereign. I think we'd better go to the station and get a proper statement drawn up.'

The woman and her friend were reluctant to accompany him but he persuaded them that it was necessary and they went out and down the road in company.

'I don't know what people will think if they see me walking down the street with a policeman,' said the woman.

He made no reply and they went on until, turning a corner he suddenly found himself confronted by the pickpocket himself. 'Well, well!' he gasped. 'This is lucky for us!'

The pickpocket was pinned against the wall and hand-cuffed in a moment. He tried to struggle but P.C. Williams wasn't to be hauled away very easily and a sudden jerk pulled the offender onto his toes.

'Gently now,' said the policeman. 'I don't want to pull you on your back all the way to the station, do I? You wouldn't like it and your coat would probably wear out before I got you there!'

The two women were full of admiration. The one who had lost her purse wanted to go through the prisoner's pockets at once and the young policeman found himself trying to explain to her why this could not be done. Her companion was one for rough and ready justice and swung her bag and brought it down on the pickpocket's head.

'I'll bray thee lug for thee!' she threatened. 'Th'art a dirty thief!'

The bag came up again in a full-blooded swing and it was all that P.C. Williams could do to prevent it reaching its target a second time.

'Look,' he said, 'you better stop that or I'll have to take you in as well!'

The threat left the woman speechless. She stood back and regarded the constable and his prisoner with distaste.

'Who stole my friend's bloody purse?' she yelled. 'Who are thee to stop us bashing him if we've a mind to?'

He almost laughed. There was little he could say in the face of such female fury. All at once the sixpence was as important as a sovereign.

'Now behave yourself,' he said.

The pickpocket tried to look out from beneath the cap which the bag had driven down over his eyes.

'You goin' t'stop this or not?' he demanded.

'I'll stop it!' promised his captor and began to run him along the pavement so fast that the two women had to run to keep up with the long strides the policeman was taking.

The arrest caused another stir at the station. Taffy, the Welshman, caught a thief. He was angry about the way they brought that up and as soon as he was free he hurried back to the hall to see the young woman who had pinned the flower on his tunic. Even the flower had come in for attention, but he had dragged it out of sight before the sergeant spotted it.

The hall was empty. He looked about at the stacked trestles and the few odds and ends of unsold items piled in a corner. She had gone and he would never see her again! He was about to turn away when the caretaker came through from a small room at one side.

'Well, well,' he said. 'I hear you caught that man after all.'

'I'm looking for the young woman who was on the stall here,' he said, pointing to the floor.

'What's she done then? Stolen something?'

Years afterwards he remembered that. She had in a way but it was hardly a matter for a report.

'I thought she might be a good witness,' he said a little lamely.

The caretaker winked at him. 'I shouldn't be surprised, but you're not in luck, are you? She comes from Accrington. Now if you like to see the minister he can tell you. You see, his brother is her minister there. He could give you the address.'

It didn't put him off at all. He went round to the minister's house and inquired.

'You could write care of my brother,' said the minister smiling. 'I am sure he will contact Miss Stafford when he knows that it is a police inquiry.'

They looked at each other for a moment and P.C. Williams found himself colouring. 'Well sir,' he said, 'I really shouldn't make that my excuse. As a matter of fact sir, the young lady pinned a flower on my uniform and I was very taken with her . . .'

'I understand. I'll drop my brother a line just the same, and you call by and I'll let you know.'

He shook hands with the minister and took himself off to the section house thinking that he was a probationer with a while to serve before he would be on a constable's full pay, and what was more he had planned to go back home. It was all the more complicated when he thought that Mary Ellen Stafford lived in Accrington, which wasn't exactly a suburb of Manchester.

In due course he called on the minister and was given the address. Mary Ellen Stafford lived at 64 Garbett Street, Accrington, care of Whittaker.

Fate is one way of explaining what may otherwise be complete and extraordinary chance. As Arthur Howell Williams sat down to write to his Mary Ellen the young lady herself was thinking of him and wondering why it was his straight-backed figure seemed so familiar to her. It seemed that she already knew him well. She had seen him before. She carried a vague recollection of his lean features in her mind and she had never been to Manchester before and never visited Wales. There had been no time for them to become acquainted. All the way back to Accrington she had talked to her friend Annie Whittaker about the young policeman and Annie had smiled and taken a delight in the romance the two of them saw in the brief encounter.

'I know him, too,' said Annie. 'It'll come to me. You wait. I'll remember!'

Annie didn't remember, but had she walked down a certain street in Accrington the picture of a soldier on horseback would surely have brought enlightenment. Gallantly upright and proud, Yeoman Arthur Howell Williams, seated on the colonel's finest mount advertised the lithographic skill of an Accrington firm of printers who had been commissioned to do an advertising poster for the Shropshire Volunteer Force. As smart as any in his detachment, eighteen-year-old Arthur Howell Williams had been chosen as the model. He had been compelled to sit very still. The colonel's horse had been one of the steadiest animals that could be found for the purpose and the photographer whose work had resulted in the extraordinary colour reproduction had had no trouble. The uniform tunic was blue, the red-braided breeches, white. Wearing a fine peaked cap and a shining leather bandolier and Sam Browne belt Yeoman Williams's portrait had impressed many a young fellow, who saw himself similarly mounted, wearing the bright chain epaulettes and spurs with the rifle in its scabbard close to hand. No one in Accrington was likely to take himself off to the Welsh marches to enlist in the volunteers, of course, but the printers had been so impressed with the quality of their own work that they had decided to use the poster to encourage similar business in Lancashire. Annie Whittaker, who was already married, had sighed and agreed with Mary Ellen that the young volunteer was smart and handsome enough to turn any young woman's head. Either young woman would surely have recognized their yeoman had he been wearing something other than the blue uniform of the police, but Yeoman Williams, weekend volunteer, had pulled up his roots and travelled out of Wales, leaving behind not only the trappings of Yeomanry but the less colourful uniform of the Post Office, whose service he had found unexciting, to say the least.

The encounter in the church hall was followed by others. P.C. Williams explained to the young woman who had stolen his heart that he had no more than fifty shillings a week to offer her and nowhere to live except rooms. He would even have to notify his superiors of his intention to marry, if she would have him, and they would have to be satisfied that she was the right sort of young woman to be a policeman's wife; not that this would affect his intention to marry her if she would have him. What it really meant was that if the higher officers found the slightest reason against his marriage he would have no alternative but to resign. The wages of fifty shillings depended on many things. A constable might be dismissed for smiling at the wrong moment. Discipline was strict. A man whose face didn't fit would be walking the street out of uniform without the chance of an appeal. There were no agitators. There was no overtime. Duty began on the minute of the hour but a constable might be required to remain on duty for as long as his superior thought fit. It was not an easy life for the man who had been sworn in but it was just as hard for the woman who married him. No one really trusted a policeman and his wife was expected to be as loyal to the service as she was to her husband, which meant that they had no friends outside. All this P.C. Williams explained to his intended. She listened and smiled at him when he told her how it was and how it had been for his father and mother and his father's brothers, who were also in the police.

'Will you marry me then, *del?*' he asked.

'I will,' she said. 'And we'll get out of this dirty place as soon as we can.'

He laughed and kissed her. She was a woman in a thousand, a strong, happy woman who had been brought up by her grandparents after her mother had died. Her father had departed for India, to die in his turn, leaving her orphaned and dominated by grandparents for whom she could conjure up little affection. She had been brought up in north Lancashire but her blood ties were with Cumberland. Cumberland, the young Welshman told her, was the land of the *cwms* or *cwymriland*—almost a part of Wales! Mary Ellen took his word for it. Indeed, she might easily have passed for a dark-haired, round-faced young Welshwoman, although it was a good few years before she spoke Welsh well enough for her 'naturalization' to be complete.

They were married at Wesley Chapel, Abbey Street, Accrington, on the sixteenth of July of the following year, 1908, Annie Whittaker, Mary Ellen's dressmaker friend, and her husband John, acting as witnesses. For the purpose of the Marriage Act Arthur Howell Williams established residence next door to his intended bride. They had neither time nor money for a honeymoon and returned to Manchester to live in rooms. A year later, their first child, a daughter, was born. P.C. Williams sat down, at last, to write to his father about getting back home to Wales.

'What do you think,' he wrote, 'about my applying to the Chief Constable at Dolgellau, to see if I can get taken on in Merioneth? I don't want to inflict this place on our children. Mary Ellen agrees with me that we must get out of here. You wouldn't believe how bad the fog is and how black and dirty the place is. I have been a probationer here. I think that having had training in the big city my experience of police work might be appreciated. I would send details of my commendations and the Chief Constable could take up my record with the Manchester Force. I see no future here, not because I am young and would have to wait for older men to have their turn, but because I know I will die in this place if I have to stay here.'

His father wrote back by return. Since he had no furniture, and the three of them could move without trouble, he must come home for as long as it took to get things straightened out. A word with someone in the neighbouring force was being conveyed to Dolgellau. A telegram would follow.

The telegram came one morning when P.C. Williams had just come off duty. Sergeant Williams hadn't been extravagant. 'Return home welcomed' was his message. Dutifully P.C. Williams returned to the station, asked for the requisite form, and filled it up.

'Trouble, Taffy?' they asked.

He shook his head. 'Not really,' he said, 'but I got to go home, and that's all there is to it.'

It wasn't quite all, of course. He was called upon for an explanation. He stood to attention and gave it.

'I want to go back to Wales, sir, and be a village policeman, like my father, and my brothers. That's the way our family is, sir. We're fond of Wales and the country.'

'You won't get far among shepherds and quarrymen,' said the inspector. 'You realize that, don't you? You can hardly compare a village policeman's work with the experience a City Force man gets. You learn more in a week here than you will in a year in the country. A village policeman is like a gravedigger, lad!'

He could have argued, but he didn't. Whatever else he was, he was a policeman who knew when to keep his mouth shut. He understood the meaning of discipline. There were other things he understood too, of course, like the smugness and arrogance of some town-dwellers. A country policeman's life was quiet, and not always exactly dramatic, but the work required just as careful study of the minds of men as it did in the city. Country people were no less cunning, no less devious than town people. They taught a policeman just as much as any city law-breaker. It was a cat-and-mouse game wherever it was played. He wanted to practise his calling among his own people, in a place he knew and loved and Mary Ellen was content to come with him. In fact she wanted it as much as he did.

He handed in his warrant, his uniform and truncheon on the due date, and hurried home to escort Mary Ellen and their daughter to the station. When they crossed the border into Wales, he was happier than he had been for years. *Hiraeth* was something he didn't know again until 1916, when he went to France.

Sergeant Williams welcomed the young Englishwoman warmly and everyone spoke English out of politeness, in the characteristic way of Welsh people. Thus far Mary Ellen had picked up only a very few words of Welsh and her knowledge of it amused her husband rather than impressed him.

'You'll have to learn more of it,' he told her, 'because we may be stationed in places where they don't speak English at all! What will you say when they can't understand you, girl, eh? No good talking to them in English, and all you know in Welsh is bad language!'

It wasn't true, but Arthur Howell's sense of humour was well-developed. He loved to pull her leg. Before she learnt the language he was to have many a laugh at her expense.

'You need waste no time,' said Sergeant Williams, 'but sit down and make application to see the Chief Constable at Dolgellau. You'll be sent for for an interview. It's up to you. Make yourself as smart as you can. Your Mam will press your clothes and clean your boots so you're presentable—'

'There will be no need for any of that,' said Mary Ellen. 'I am the one to make him presentable, Mr Williams! I'll attend to his clothes and I'll clean his boots!'

Sergeant Williams hastily withdrew. Mary Ellen looked at her husband and smiled. She didn't remind him that she was a dressmaker and quite as competent with her needle as any woman in Wales. She would see that his suit was renovated.

The journey to the county town involved a long walk over the mountain, and many a lift begged on the way from carriers and carters. Arthur Howell Williams stood at last before the Chief Constable, his head up, his cap held between finger and thumb of his right hand as he came to attention. The Chief Constable looked through the papers and cleared his throat. He was about to ask a question on the Night Poaching Act of 1828, something a little outside the knowledge of a city constable!

3
Country Beat

OCCURRENCE BOOK ENTRY:

It has been reported that sheep thought to have been stolen from James Roberts, Tan y Bwlch Farm, are being slaughtered and sold by Richard Elias Hughes, Pen y Bont, and fleeces of same sold to Thomas Wynne Parry, Tannery, Ffestiniog.

HE returned to Llansilin a great deal quicker than he had gone, it seemed. Certainly his step was much lighter, for the Chief Constable had expressed his satisfaction with the information he had been given. 'Well, Williams,' he had said, 'I think there's a place for you at Ffestiniog. We can make use of you there immediately. Pity your wife doesn't speak Welsh, but maybe she can learn it. I know your father and one of your brothers serving in Denbighshire. Your brother in Shropshire has a good record there.' Well enough. But it would take a while for Mary Ellen to learn Welsh, maybe longer than it would take her to settle in in a little stone house in Ffestiniog. They wouldn't have much, but they would gather what they could. They were due in Blaenau Ffestiniog on the twenty-eighth of the month, a day, when it didn't fall on a Sunday, policemen expected to move if they had to. Mary Ellen wouldn't fret much about things getting wet as they were carted from one house to another. There would be hardly anything to be carted, whether it rained or shined.

It shone, however. The sky bluer than blue and the singing larks were high when P.C. Williams and his wife left his father's house to go to Blaenau Ffestiniog. They had only a few items to carry, a bundle of blankets and some towels and sheets which they could trust the carrier to look after when he stopped to load and unload packages and parcels along the way. While they were waiting for the carrier Arthur saw his mother hurrying down to them. She had a parcel under her arm and she thrust it into Mary Ellen's hand and told her to take care of it. Mary Ellen knew it was a picture. She smiled at her mother-in-law and said at least they would have something to put on the wall of that cold, bare house in Blaenau. The carrier arrived and the picture was handed up along with their bundle. Mary Ellen transferred the baby from one arm to the other and prepared herself for the journey. No one spoke to them on the way, for they were so obviously wrapped in their own thoughts. The young policeman talked quietly to his wife and baby. He was at home, and she was in a strange country, but neither of them knew quite how life would be in the Vale of Ffestiniog where his beat would lie.

'You begin by letting them see that you favour nobody,' he had been told by his father. 'You've been in Manchester, all right, but don't be clever with them. You sort the sheep from the goats in a little while and they'll sort you from the kind of man that was there before you.'

The journey took longer than they had expected. They were anxious to be in Blaenau in time to buy a bed, a mattress, some chairs and a table, as well as the household things they needed for cooking. The stone house was like every other stone house in the locality, roofed with Ffestiniog slate, built of the rock of the locality. It had no piped water and its rear windows were overshadowed by the mountain. Mary Ellen sniffed the damp and hurried to get a fire lit. The dealer from whom they had bought their bits of furniture came hurrying up with his handcart. In next to no time the bed was in place in one room, the table and chairs in another, and Mary Ellen improvised curtains from some material she had bought.

'It doesn't look so bad,' said her husband, looking at the fire smoking and the faded marks on the wall.

'It will look better in time,' said Mary Ellen. 'Unwrap that picture and hang it on the nail.'

P.C. Williams obeyed. Mary Ellen was too busy to admire the first decorative touch put to the drabness of a grey, damp police house. She was cooking ham and eggs and preparing to feed her daughter.

'I hope she sleeps,' she remarked, remembering how well the child had slept on the carrier's cart.

Her husband had found the things his predecessor had left for him, papers concerning inquiries he had been making, a blunt pencil and a tattered jotter.

'Drunk and riotous, drunk and riotous, drunk and riotous,' he said. 'Wet outside, and wet in, that seems to be Blaenau Ffestiniog!' He was forgetting that for once Blaenau was bathed in the warmth of the setting sun, and gloomy though the house was a shaft of sunlight fell on the wall, lighting up the figure of Mary Ellen as she worked.

'It's not wet, anyway,' said Mary Ellen and then she broke off, staring at the wall. 'It's you! It's you!' she gasped.

Arthur looked at the picture of himself in the uniform of the Shropshire Yeomanry.

'It's me,' he confessed. 'What about it, then?'

She turned to him with her eyes bright and a smile wreathing her face as she spoke. 'I knew it,' she said. 'I knew I'd seen you before! That picture was in the window in Accrington! Annie and I stood and admired it long before I ever saw you!'

'There then,' he said. 'A wanted poster! Reward offered for information leading to the capture of the above-named, Arthur Howell Williams, at one time a member of the Shropshire Yeomanry, thought to be in the Accrington district!'

They laughed and Mary Ellen went over and studied her yeoman and made her husband stand beside his portrait so that he could be compared with himself at eighteen.

'Not quite such a boy,' she said.

'Armed and maybe dangerous,' said the policeman.

It wasn't until the following day that he reported for duty and stood to attention, anxious not to put a foot wrong.

'All right, Williams, you're not in Manchester!' said the sergeant smiling. 'All I want to know is, did you read what Hughes left for you and are you familiar with his inquiries about sheep that James Roberts lost?'

'I'm ready to go, Sergeant,' he said. 'Is it far?'

'It's as far as you'll walk,' said the sergeant, 'and just as far on a bicycle.'

'I'll walk, if that's the best. Tell me where the place is. The wife will give me some bread and cheese to keep me going.'

'Not today, Williams. Not today! Anybody might guess you been in Manchester! This is Sunday, Williams. You won't get anywhere on a Sunday. Good and bad are in chapel, aren't they?'

The following morning, armed with a map which the sergeant had made, and carrying his lunch in his pocket, P.C. Williams set off to make inquiries about sheep-stealing on the mountain. He passed the corner where the carrier's cart had dropped them, and tramped on along the quiet, early-morning road. How different it was to walk a country beat, to see the cattle in the fields and hear the streams tumbling down the gulleys and ravines that cut into the sides of the mountain. Sheep were everywhere. He knew that they strayed, intermingled, got lost and, inevitably, got stolen. It wasn't an easy complaint to investigate. His father had often bemoaned the fact that sheep-stealing came next to illegitimacy in the list of baffling things with which a policeman might find himself concerned. Unmarked lambs were gathered and marked, despite the fact that the ewe might belong to another flock. If the sheep were separated on the mountain while the lamb was still suckling the indications were that someone had either been careless at marking time, or had tried to increase his flock at the expense of his neighbour. If the segregation of the flocks took place later on, at dipping or shearing time, it sometimes happened that the 'stolen' lamb had become independent of its mother. The true owner could only speculate about the number of ewes he had lambed and the number of yearlings he was likely to have in the end. The case of James Roberts's sheep was a little different, however. It seemed that his sheep were being killed and the head or shoulder markings cut away from the fleeces. The suspect was a man whose reputation had never been very good. It was the policeman's task to get to the bottom of things and P.C. Williams was determined to do that. Catching a rogue in Blaenau was surely not harder than catching one in Manchester?

'You have come, then,' said the owner of the sheep, 'to ask me the same old questions, teh? The man who was here before you, and your sergeant know well enough who killed my sheep, and where the fleeces of them are!'

'If I don't ask my own questions,' said P.C. Williams, 'and think about the answers, how can I catch anybody? Now how many sheep can you gather up for me?'

The farmer scratched his head. 'I can catch as many as

you need! What is catching them going to do? You think you can tell a sheep after it is slaughtered and skinned?'

The young policeman cleared his throat and spoke very slowly and gently. 'I'm not that clever, Mr Roberts, but I got an idea. If you catch up twenty or thirty sheep of the quality and age you been losing, we could put a special mark on the fleece . . .'

'Indeed! Indeed! We could do that, but what will Hughes do? He'll trim the fleece like he did before, and nobody will know. You should think longer. Such a thing would be a waste of my time and yours!'

'I thought all the way here, Mr Roberts,' said the policeman. 'I think we could beat him, and catch him red-handed, but you got to lose a few more sheep before he goes to prison, just one more lot.'

'One way I could stop him,' said the angry farmer. 'I could catch him in the act and blow a hole in his head with my gun!'

'There won't be need for anything like that. You gather your sheep. Get your wife to let us have a reel of the best white thread she has. We'll get a needle and put a length of thread through the tail of every one of those sheep, see?'

The farmer's anger vanished. He looked up at the tall young policeman and beamed at him.

'You're not a fool, boy,' he said. 'You've got brains! We'll catch him this time!'

'We will, because you'll tell me when you miss the sheep, and I'll tell the tannery to let me know as soon as the suspect brings the fleeces in. They'll be set on one side, identified. We'll have him!'

It was the next day that the marking was done and P.C. Williams had to make another long tramp to the farm. The farmer had brought a reliable witness who was sworn to secrecy and watched the cotton being threaded through the tails of the sheep. It was a slow and tiring business. When it was done the young policeman looked ruefully at his muddied and woolly uniform as he sat eating his bread and cheese by the sheepfold.

They would have laughed at him in Manchester, he was sure of that. He would have been pulled up for the state of his uniform, told to make himself fit to be seen— and get his boots polished!

'You married?' asked the farmer.

He said he was, and almost as soon as he said it the farmer's wife came bustling across the courtyard to present him with a dozen eggs. He flushed and hesitated.

'You know,' he said, 'I'm new in Blaenau and not long in the Police Force. I am not well paid, but I can't take them. You know what it is, thank you, *diolch yn fawr.*'

He stood up, shook hands with the farmer, and bade him good afternoon. They smiled at each other.

A day or two later, coming in from the street, Mary Ellen found a bag of eggs on her doorstep. There was no message. She mentioned it to her husband. He shrugged his shoulders. He had heard about laying-away hens, but they didn't nest in paperbags.

At the tannery P.C. Williams was received with a touch of anxiety. He guessed that perhaps they knew more about sheep-stealing and the perfidious ways of dealers than he would ever discover.

'I want you to get in touch with me the very next time Mr Richard Elias Hughes, Pen Bont, comes here with sheepskins. I want you to put those skins under lock and key at once, and let no one else see them or touch them. They will be marked skins. I have reason to believe it will not be very long before skins are brought.'

The tannery owner frowned. 'How are these skins marked?' he asked.

'I can only tell you that they are marked, and warn

you not to reveal what I have told you in case such a disclosure assisted someone in committing a felony.'

He had phrased the caution carefully. Even the sergeant had been compelled to admit that the plan was something he himself wouldn't have thought of. If it worked the Chief would hear about it, that was certain.

For three, and then four and five weeks, there was no news. P.C. Williams walked his beat, checked the way a horse's harness rubbed its flanks, moved a tramp from a haystack to the Union, carried messages, looked in the alehouse door when voices were raised, and went to church on Sunday, dressed in his uniform. The place was beginning to know him. Tall as a tree, they said he was, the long fellow. Some of the harder men in Blaenau were tempted to see if he was able to take care of himself, or whether he was just another big fellow in a uniform. He gave them no occasion to put him to the test, but he was there when they came stumbling along the unlit street on a Saturday night. Certainly it couldn't be said that he was avoiding trouble.

'No news?' the sergeant would ask. There had been other entries since the one he had made about sheep with marks on their tails.

'If those sheep are stolen and the fleeces brought to the tannery we'll know who stole them,' he said confidently.

Mary Ellen listened to what he said. She hoped that he would be successful. He needed to establish himself in the place, to earn a little credit, acquire a reputation. She prayed that the sheep-stealer would fall into her young husband's trap before much longer. No one could subsist on hope for ever. There was a time for sowing, the bible said, and a time for reaping, if it could be put that way!

It was the month of August before the trap was sprung. One evening when Arthur and Mary had gone to bed there was a knock at the door. Arthur fumbled for his trousers and couldn't find them in the gloom, and the knock was repeated.

'Who is there?' he asked in Welsh.

'Roberts, Tan Bwlch,' came the reply.

He opened the door and admitted the caller, even although he was hardly dressed to receive official visitors.

'Well?' he said, standing tall and white in his vest and long woollen drawers.

'The sheep have gone, eight of them! They were there this afternoon when I was looking them over, and when I went back this evening they were gone. They haven't just strayed. They're gone. He's got them. You better get to the tannery in the morning, teh?'

Williams scratched himself and thought about that. The sheep would have to be killed and skinned. Time enough to go to the tannery when word came that fleeces had been brought in.

'I'll go when they send for me,' he said. 'Wouldn't do for him to know I was calling there before he brought the fleeces, would it?'

The little farmer reached up and clapped him on the shoulder.

'I'd never make a policeman, would I?' he said. 'You're right again, and you'll catch him!'

'Thanks for coming,' said Williams, letting his visitor back out on to the sleepy, empty street.

'What was that then?' Mary Ellen asked sleepily.

She was soon to have their second child and she needed her rest.

'I'll tell you in the morning,' he promised. 'You just start counting sheep.'

In the morning he told the sergeant. The thing was going to be put to the test now. Sergeant Evans blew into his ragged moustache. He was going to be there when Elias Hughes was confronted with his crime. For far too long he had been getting away with this kind of thing. Justice was justice. He had it coming!

There was no news from the tannery. It seemed that someone had mentioned an official visit and the sheep-stealer was resigned to losing the small amount he might make from the fleeces.

'Patience, Williams,' said Sergeant Evans. 'Your Dad told you you got to have patience in our job, didn't he? I know Elias Hughes. He has no rind on his cheese."

The young policeman understood. Elias ate both the cheese and the rind. He was a greedy man. He wouldn't forgo the price of the fleeces if he had slaughtered and sold the sheep, and he couldn't keep them too long in August. They would be riddled with maggot and no use at all if he delayed.

That afternoon a small boy came down the street while P.C. Williams was watching a tramp making his way into one of the backyard alleys.

'Please, I was to tell you that Mr Parry wants to see you as soon as you can call.'

He patted the little fellow on the head and went up the street. By chance Sergeant Evans was cycling down the street at that very moment. He held up his hand. The sergeant turned his bicycle and wobbled over to stop beside him.

'Parry has just sent me word to come. The fleeces must be there,' he said.

The tannery hummed with the sound of bluebottles. The air reeked of skins going rotten, of decaying flesh, of sheep droppings and oily wool, to say nothing of the smell of the vats. The two policemen took a gulp of air and felt sick.

'The fleeces were brought to me half an hour ago,' said Parry, who both ran and owned the yard. 'I gave him a receipt for them. They are still tied in the bag I

put them back in when I took them from him, his bag.
They all have his mark on them, though. I think you
made a mistake.'

'This couldn't be any other bag but his?'

'This is the only bag. It's got his label on it, look,
Hughes, Pen Bont. I'll open it for you.'

'Open it and lay the fleeces out on that table, one
beside the other,' said P.C. Williams.

Parry complied with the order. Sergeant Evans watched
his colleague take a pencil and move the wool on each
fleece, inspecting the tail and ignoring a blue brand that
had obviously not been long applied.

P.C. Williams took out his notebook and looked at his
sergeant.

'I'll make a receipt for these, Sergeant,' he said. 'If
Mr Parry cares to hold the bag as I put them in.'

The tannery owner caught his breath and looked from
one to the other. 'I'm not involved in anything,' he said.
'I took them with his mark on them! I want that understood!'

'You've got nothing to worry about if that's the case,'
said Sergeant Evans, 'but I warn you to tell me anything
you know. P.C. Williams marked certain fleeces. These
are the first to turn up.'

The young policeman said nothing. All at once he
understood that the old sergeant wasn't so dull. He was
frightening the tannery owner.

'You take fleeces with the neck cut or trimmed where
there might be marks?' he asked.

'Sometimes. If a fleece is torn, cut, holed, I trim it.
Sometimes the man who butchers the sheep trims it.'

'You get half a dozen at a time?'

Parry said nothing. He could see where the thing
might lead.

'All right,' said the sergeant. 'We've got something
more important to do just now, but we'll be back.'

Outside on the road P.C. Williams borrowed the sergeant's bicycle so that the large sack of fleeces could be transported down the street. They were watched on their way to the police station.

'It'll be all over the place before we even bring him in,' said the sergeant. 'But one thing you can be sure of, there won't be much sheep-stealing for a while! If there is, they'll burn the skins.'

P.C. Williams thought about it as he took the evil-smelling bundle through to the yard and the shed at the back. Sheep couldn't be identified except by their marks, marks on their heads, flanks, backs, clips or perforations in their ears. These marks were known to the owners but only to them and their immediate neighbours. It seemed a pity that there was no register of marks kept by dealers, butchers, the police. He wondered how it could be done. It was something that the sergeant or the inspector might put up to the 'big man', whoever he was.

'Well, Williams,' said the sergeant. 'You've arrested a man before. I don't need to remind you how you go about it, I hope?'

They set out for Pen y Bont, keeping in step with each other, the sergeant puffing a little on the hills. He had left his bicycle behind. He had his staff and handcuffs with him. Richard Elias Hughes was a notoriously violent man and might need to be restrained. The sergeant didn't tell his junior this. He wanted to see how he would react in an emergency if one arose. So far he had used his head. Soon, perhaps, he would have to use his hands.

'You are Richard Elias Hughes?' said P.C. Williams when at last they stood at the door of Pen y Bont farm.

Richard Elias Hughes nodded his head. His eyes had a wary look. Standing behind the young constable, Sergeant Evans prepared to back him up. He could read the signs immediately.

'I believe you took some sheepskins to the tannery at Ffestiniog about mid-day today?'

'I did,' said Hughes. 'What about it?'

'They were marked with blue marks.'

'My marks.'

'I have reason to believe that they were the skins of sheep taken from Tan y Bwlch Farm and were the property of James Roberts.'

'You and James Roberts are bloody liars!'

P.C. Williams saw the blow coming but wasn't able to dodge it before it grazed his ear. His helmet slipped and tumbled from his head, but he reached out and caught his assailant's arm and quickly locked it against his shoulder.

'I think you better come to the station and make a statement!' he said breathlessly. 'You can hear the charge there!'

'All right, Williams,' said the sergeant, stepping closer. 'We'll just secure him in case he wants to repeat the offence. The first charge could be sheep-stealing, the second could be assaulting a police officer. We could say resisting arrest if we go any further. Maybe you better warn him.'

No one came out of the house. Richard Elias Hughes's family had retreated somewhere within. He neither called to them nor looked back as he accompanied the two policemen down the rough road and into Blaenau. On the way P.C. Williams avoided the eyes of the cottagers and passers-by paused to see the arrested man being taken in. It was a very quiet countryside but people were just as full of curiosity as they were in Manchester.

'It's that new policeman in 'Stiniog,' they said. 'Walks like a wolf, he does. Taking 'Lias away like he didn't know he's a ruffian and would break your jaw soon as look at you!'

'Lias wasn't being given a chance to demonstrate his

ferocity. In fact his ferocity had deserted him. He had an uneasy feeling that he was not coming back along the road as quickly as he might have done had he avoided robbing James Roberts of another batch of sheep.

'The sheep were ingeniously marked by P.C. Williams,' said the prosecutor at the trial. 'Watch was kept but when they were stolen P.C. Williams had to wait some time before the accused brought the fleeces to the tannery of Mr Parry. It was a remarkably watertight device and the accused could not deny that he had taken the fleeces to the tannery or that he had marked them with his own mark. What he couldn't get over was that they were already marked, not just on the neck with the mark of James Roberts, a mark which he found no difficulty in trimming off, but on the tails with a strong and distinctively knotted length of cotton, something neither he nor the unsuspecting purchaser could have discovered without most careful examination. I need only say that the witnesses have confirmed the evidence of the arresting officers.'

P.C. Williams sat waiting for the sentence. Richard Elias Hughes had asked for other offences to be taken into account, it seemed. He had not been mistaken. The Vale of Ffestiniog was to miss his shadow for three months, during which time he did hard labour.

In Ffestiniog they watched P.C. Williams with renewed interest. He was no fool. In fact, he was a policeman to look out for. He was more than a long fellow, he was a long-headed fellow. There was more under his helmet than a bone head. Look how he had sorted out Elias Hughes! A lively policeman was one thing, but here was one who was cunning, crafty, a fellow to be watched! They took sides, of course, and some loved him for his cleverness. Some hated him for the same reason. He had sorted out the sheep-stealer, and he was sorting the sheep from the goats as his father had prophesied he would.

It was inevitable that the inspector would talk to him about the success of his first case.

'Right then, Williams,' he said. 'That's one for the book. A good start. You got to keep the thing moving, however. The way a place behaves reflects the way the policeman stationed there behaves. Sheep-stealing is one thing, but what about drunk and riotous behaviour? What about tramps that sleep out everywhere from here to Penrhyndeudraeth? What about the little lot you got camping on the roadside?'

'I'm out, sir,' he said. 'I'm after them.'

'Not enough, Williams. Bring them in!'

He stood to attention, listening to the lecture and decided that it wasn't the time to suggest a register of sheep ear-marks. It wouldn't do to write to the Super, or anyone higher up, until the inspector approved.

'Well,' said Mary Ellen. 'What did the inspector have to say?'

He sat down and began to eat his tea:

'He said I should be out catching the gipsies, the tramps and the drunks. One swallow doesn't make a summer!'

She patted his shoulder. 'Never mind, you'll show them.'

He hadn't the heart to tell her something else the inspector had hinted at. They were barely settled but the chances were that he would be moved from Blaenau. The inspector hadn't said where, but he knew something. He had seen the book, somewhere. One of the higher-ups, who played draughts with policemen and their families, had decided that Williams was in line for a move. That was all, and there was no appeal.

Elizabeth was almost exactly a year old when their second child, a boy, christened David Moelwyn, was born. Perhaps the higher-up who had let the inspector see the book relented. They weren't moved that year, but when their third child, named Arthur Leslie was born they were in Tanygrisau, a few miles away, in a little stone house with the words County Police Station on it. It was January 1913. They were more of a family, better-known in the locality, and more comfortable at home, although now there were five mouths to feed, three more than when they married. Arthur Howell Williams earned less than sixty shillings a week and bought all his own clothing with the exception of tunic, helmet and greatcoat. If the village policeman's lot wasn't exactly an unhappy one he was far from well off. There wasn't a penny to spare. Mrs Williams often had to make soup from nettles.

4

Cock Crow and Hen Cackle

OCCURRENCE BOOK ENTRY:

I was present when my wife searched the accused. On her person she was found to be wearing a petticoat with a special pocket. In this pocket a fowl was found. She admitted stealing fowls from the shed of Mr Charles Morris. She said my husband made me steal them.

TANYGRISAU, the first of a succession of postings that were to mark the years of his service like milestones, was a backwater in the stream, quiet, so that if a cock crowed at any time of day it could be heard in any of the houses of the village. If a dog barked those who belonged in the place knew whose dog it was and could picture that dog in the backyard of the terrace. Nothing much happened in the little place, but P.C. Williams was stationed there to take care of things that concerned the police and authority in general. His beat was larger than the village and a great deal longer than it had been in Blaenau. He was officer in charge, a sort of headman in the village, and in all cases of dispute the villagers came to him. They brought him more than their complaints. They brought their fears, told him of a wayward son or daughter, a drunken husband, the furtive behaviour of a neighbour. They confessed and they informed, ingratiated themselves as far as they were able, and looked for the policeman's goodwill and sympathy. Arthur Howell contended with it all as best he could. His confessor was his wife. He had no one else in whom he could confide. She listened to his problems, the problems of the village, and they talked them over together—the thing to do about a known thief, a man who beat or betrayed his wife, a youth who seduced a minor, or was suspected of having committed the offence, and the problem of chicken thieves.

The theft of fowls was one of those offences that had cluttered up the Occurrence Book from the very earliest days of the constabulary. It featured on the petty sessional records away back beyond the generation of Marwood the hangman and Charlie Peace. It was a crime for which the magistrates at petty sessions might sentence an offender to hard labour for fourteen or twenty-one days. Like drunkenness, there were seasons when the complaint was more prevalent. Tramps stole fowls. Poor and hungry people seized a chicken when it strayed on a field or was encountered on the road. Villains stole fowls from Michaelmas to Christmas, as they still do today. The village policeman was expected to apprehend his fair quota of offenders. His task might involve staying out of bed as cockerels crowed to the moon until at last they welcomed the coming of a new day. When the Occurrence Book was checked the inspecting officer looked for names and the note that So-and-So had been charged.

'Williams,' said the inspector when he called on him a few weeks before Christmas 1914, 'I can't say you're not doing well, but you've got to stop some of the fowl-stealing before the "big man" comes to look at the book, so you get out keeping watch. Catch somebody!'

As always, P.C. Williams nodded respectfully. No one caught a chicken thief by looking in the cooking pots.

It was a little more subtle than that. A policeman had to have a good idea who stole fowls. He had to be pretty certain that he was engaged in stealing them and make a shrewd guess where he would commit his next offence. There was only one sort of thief worth catching, the habitual thief. The beginner might commit a crime successfully once. The second or third time, in the simple process of gaining experience, he would do something wrong and get caught by accident.

'Very good, sir,' he said. 'I'll watch. I think I can lay my hands on one.'

He said it the way he might once have told his mother that if she needed something for dinner he was pretty sure he knew where he could shoot or snare a pheasant, as long as Dad didn't know.

The sergeant was busy signing papers when the inspector took his leave.

'You keep observation, Arthur. If anything turns up you meet me at the crossroad at twelve,' he remarked.

Sergeant Nicholas made his rounds on his bicycle, meeting the village constables at night at certain quiet places where he and they could exchange information and cope with problems that might have arisen. Most of the time these meetings were little more than an occasion for gossip. The Vale of Ffestiniog was generally quiet and for weeks on end nothing happened. Crime, however, has a rhythm that has always been noted by discerning police officers.

On P.C. Williams's beat the tramps had been flushed from the outhouses and shepherded away to the warmer confines of the lock-up or the workhouse, but now he was going to have to stand and wait in one of those cold and draughty barns, wait for one of the villagers, or some labourer from one of the farms, to help himself to a few hens, ducks or geese.

'Moonrise to cockcrow,' he said heavily, buttoning the

top button of his greatcoat and looking at Mary Ellen as she inquired when he would be back.

'Who will you book?' she inquired.

'It's Will Chickens,' he said.

The Welsh people have an apt way of conferring nicknames on members of their community that is unequalled anywhere else. A man's nickname can never be shaken off. At some time he earned it. On occasions the nickname serves as a warning to those who hear it. Will Chickens had been convicted for stealing fowls again and again. He was the policeman's natural choice.

'I've seen rubbish burning in his yard,' said the policeman as he stood drinking the tea his wife had made. 'Feathers, dampened and stuffed in sacks. He's busy. I know where he's been stealing. I've got to guess where he'll do it next. I've picked my place, and I'll keep watch there. I'll catch him.'

He kissed his wife on the cheek, went out on to the black village street and plodded away to the farm he expected to be visited by Will Chickens. Dogs barked and the moon rose. It was a bitterly cold night. Will Chickens must have put his nose out of doors and decided that it was too cold for him. The policeman's first night's vigil was marked by nothing more than the sight of a barn owl perched on the upright shaft of a cart in the farmyard. Sheltering in the open-sided shed, the policeman could have sworn that the owl stayed on the point of the shaft just to watch him. It flew away when cocks were crowing for dawn and a light showed in the farmhouse. P.C. Williams beat his arms against his sides and knocked on the farmhouse door. After a minute or two he was admitted by the farmer and invited to join him in a bowl of *brewas*.

'He didn't come,' P.C. Williams told his host. 'But he'll be here! Keep the dogs indoors. I'll watch until he comes.'

The second night proved more exciting. For shortly after eleven o'clock Will Chickens arrived on the scene. He walked very softly to the henhouse, trailing a sack in one hand. He made no sound getting the door open. The watching policeman waited for the cackling of the hens. They made very little sound. Will Chickens had evidently managed to get the first one without it flapping or disturbing the rest. There was something in the thief's sack when P.C. Williams laid his hand on his shoulder.

'All right, Will, that's enough,' he said. 'We don't need more than one as evidence, do we?'

Afterwards he was to squirm at the very thought of what he had said, but Will Chickens made no protest. He surrendered the sack and accompanied the policeman quietly enough. They walked down the frozen farm track to the public road and a rendezvous with Sergeant Nicholas.

'I got him,' P.C. Williams said when his sergeant came on the scene at midnight. 'One in the sack.'

The sergeant turned his bull's eye on Will Chickens's face and then directed the light on the sack.

'You seen what's in the sack then?'

It hardly seemed necessary to produce the chicken, but P.C. Williams recalled how silently it had been taken, and what little sign there had been that it really was a living thing. He opened the sack and peered into it. The bird seemed to have been waiting for that moment! With a wild cackle it burst out, beat the policeman across the eyes with its wing as it did so, and flew off into the adjoining thicket, more like a jungle bird than a domestic hen!

'Damn it!' said the sergeant. 'Damn it, Williams, get that bird back!'

But the bird had flown. It was nowhere to be found—either by moonlight or at sunrise.

'Not much use telling the magistrates that the evidence

got away! They'd throw out the whole case. Will Chickens would say he was being picked on,' said the sergeant. 'Already he says he was going to the farm to see if he could buy a few potatoes. Eleven o'clock at night? He says it was barely a quarter to ten. Can you prove it wasn't?'

P.C. Williams was downcast. 'To think I told him one was enough! I could have let him get a bagful!'

'Pity you didn't. The charge would have read better—stealing twelve fowls value thirty-six shillings, much better than one, value three shillings! You better write a report that you kept watch and interviewed a suspect but sufficient evidence was not available.'

When he told Mary Ellen she laughed at him. He frowned at first, but after a while he saw the funny side of it and laughed with her

'You can laugh,' he said. 'Sergeant Nicholas can laugh too. He's not a bad fellow, but I'm not having Will Chickens laughing! I'll catch him before too long!'

Will Chickens was caught, of course. That was inevitable, but not that season, and not the following Christmas, for by that time P.C. Williams was otherwise engaged—in France.

'You want to keep watch on that Mary Ellis at the Lion,' said one of the village gossips a few days later. 'See where she goes and what she does, teh?'

'I got a lot of things to watch and do,' he said, 'more important than watching a barmaid. I got chicken-stealing to sort out! I expect you heard that by now?'

He looked his informant straight in the eye, daring her to even smile about the way Will Chickens had escaped justice.

'That's what I mean, Mr Williams. Not all the fowls are took by Will. You keep your eye on Mrs Ellis. You'll find she believes that chickens pays, and one at a time is good fishing.'

'Now what's all this about?' he asked. 'If you got something to say, say it, and don't play about!'

'It's dark when she comes down the road past Morris's, isn't it? You heard he's losing fowls? His dog never barks. You notice what a fuss Mary Ellis makes of Morris's dog?'

'You ever seen her with a chicken?'

'Her husband sells them in Blaenau! You want to look into that and find where he gets them.'

There was nothing more to be gained from gossip. He gave no indication that he believed what he had been told. When the sergeant came he asked him to get one of the policemen in Blaenau to check if Harry Ellis had sold chickens. The word came back that he seemed to have a source of supply. He was selling them 'for a farmer's wife' who needed a few shillings before Christmas.

'I got to keep watch on that Mrs Ellis,' he told Mary Ellen when he was having his tea. 'Seems she's taking fowls, one at a time, from Morris's shed. He has them behind some netting but he can't lock the place. It's got no proper door. The dog is tied up there, but although it snarls and barks at everybody it never seems to bark when the birds are taken. Mrs Ellis has made a fuss of that dog. Her husband is selling chickens. It all adds up. What I've got to do is catch her.'

Mrs Ellis came down the street a little quicker than he would have liked. She was in the fowlhouse and out again. He was sure of that. He could see no sign of the fowl being carried away and had to be content to leave it at that, but the following day Charlie Morris told him that he had lost another bird. The tally was mounting.

'She could be hiding them up her skirt,' said Mary Ellen with a knowing smile.

He hadn't thought of that! The following evening he waited for Mrs Ellis again. She avoided him at the entrance to the fowlhouse but he hurried after her, noticing for the first time that she left a trail of feathers as she stumbled along. It wasn't until he reached the door of the Lion that he was able to catch up with the suspect.

'Mrs Ellis,' he said, 'I saw you just now, coming out of Morris's shed. I have reason to believe that you have stolen a chicken from there. You'll have to come along to the police station and be searched.'

'You won't touch me! I won't let you put your hands on me! I'll charge you!'

'My wife will search you, Mrs Ellis. I'll be present, but you have nothing to be afraid of from me.'

Mary Ellen opened the door for her husband and his prisoner.

'All right, Mary Ellen,' he said, 'I got a job for you. You'll lift this woman's skirts and see if she has a fowl in her drawers.'

Mary Ellen looked at the prisoner and then at her husband. 'I think she would be as well admitting it,' she suggested.

The prisoner flushed but said nothing. Mary Ellen lifted the barmaid's skirt and peered at her petticoat.

'Not in her drawers, Arthur,' she said. 'You needn't look away. She has a big hem on her petticoat, see? A pocket!'

Arthur watched his wife as she reached forward and brought the dead chicken out.

'What about it, then?' he asked.

The barmaid shrugged her shoulders. 'All right,' she said. 'I been taking them. Harry told me to.'

When the case was over they made fun of him. Williams looking for stolen chickens stopped at nothing. He turned women upside-down and examined their drawers, they said. He was a regular bloodhound. The jokes didn't bother him a bit for he wasn't short of a sense of fun.

'Well,' he said, 'Will Chickens beat me. I wasn't going

to let this one get away with it, even if I had to strip all her clothes off!'

Everyone laughed. Mary Ellen laughed too. She was gratified to learn that for the brief few minutes she had served the law she was regarded as a 'police matron' and for this she would receive a sum of a shilling, paid, as always in such cases, after a lapse of several months.

'You'd better arrest a few women,' Mary Ellen said. 'We could do with the money. They won't let me use my sewing machine!'

The sewing machine was in use regularly, of course. A policeman's family were expected to be turned out neat and tidy, no matter what the number of his children happened to be. Mrs Williams was skilled in the business of making and renovating clothes, but by police regulations in force at that time, and for years to come, no policeman's wife was permitted to have paid employment of any kind, or to work for anyone and receive reward of any sort. It was a hard regulation that did little to encourage a policeman to refuse gifts if these were offered by members of the public who felt a reward was due.

'I stopped a man with a salmon in a bag this morning,' P.C. Williams told his wife one lunchtime. 'He knew that I knew where it had come from, and how it was obtained. He pretended he was bringing it to me because he had found it on the river bank. I broke the law. I said to him, "Now I don't want to put all that nonsense in the book! You just get off home with it and get it cooked." He cried. He stood there and cried.'

'What was it about?' asked Mary Ellen.

'It was about a family of hungry children living with their grandad, their father in France, missing a month.'

'What would the inspector say?'

'I don't give a damn what the inspector would say! I let it go and I'd do it again. I hate to think that men like that man's sons are going every week, men with wives and children, quarrymen, roadmen, postmen. They're getting killed, hundreds of them and I'm at home!'

It was his first outburst. It wasn't to be his last. Gradually as winter gave place to spring, he found he had no enthusiasm for his duty. He plodded round the long beat with a heavy heart, thinking about the suffering of the families of men who had gone. He was a policeman and there was no obligation for him to volunteer. They would send for him if they ever needed him, said the inspector. Things at home still had to be controlled by the police. There was no change in human nature. People who had committed crimes still broke the law. The offences multiplied as food and clothing became dearer, even in small places like Blaenau.

'I see them on leave,' said Arthur to his wife. 'I don't like to look them in the face. I've got to do something! I've got you and the children, but they've got wives and children too. Nobody's going to give me a white feather. I'm going!'

Mary Ellen looked at him with anxiety and concern for his peace of mind.

'You can't just go,' she said. 'You're sworn in. You got to have permission, haven't you?'

'I have,' he said. 'I know that. I'm going to write to Dolgellau tonight! I'm going to ask the Chief Constable for his permission. I'm not going to sit back and do nothing.'

That evening he took a sheet of plain paper and wrote: 'I have the honour to serve in the Merioneth Constabulary at Tanygrisau County Police Station, to which I was posted two years ago after serving at Blaenau Ffestiniog. I respectfully ask your permission to volunteer for service in H.M. Forces and if granted will join the Royal Welsh Fusileers as soon as I am released. I know that there is a strain on manpower but I feel that I can no longer remain at home when the country is in danger.'

Mary Ellen read the letter and said nothing. After he had put it in an envelope addressed to the Chief Constable he found her quietly weeping.

'What are you crying for? You wouldn't want me to stay at home with so many others going, would you?'

'I wouldn't want you to be killed,' she said.

'I wouldn't want to be killed! Make no mistake about that! I've got to go, that's all!'

The inspector came to see him a day or two later. It seemed that the Chief Constable had been down to Blaenau.

'You've applied for your release, Williams,' he said. 'You might have told me.'

'I've applied, sir. I can't carry on. I can't take any interest in my work with the things that are happening, men being killed every day, and others coming back ruined for life.'

'The Chief Constable has a few names. He's got a problem. What happens in Merioneth when the men on the beat join up?'

'You call back the old ones, that's what you do! There must be a lot of old policemen that could be taken back.'

The inspector admitted that this was true, and in fact this solution would have to be applied throughout the country if things went on as they were doing.

P.C. Williams, to tell the truth, wasn't interested in how the Constabulary solved its problem. He only wanted to go and do his bit. In May he received a letter from Dolgellau telling him that his request had been granted. His service in the army would, for the purposes of his police pension and the record in general, count as service in the Police Force. The Chief Constable wished him well.

On the 3rd of July 1915 he was accepted into the Royal Welch Fusiliers, Private Arthur Howell Williams No. 26274, age 28, Height 5 ft 11 ins, chest 32–34 ins, weight 154 lb, enlistment at Blaenau Ffestiniog, posted to Wrexham, Denbs. By the time he went to France he had been promoted to the rank of corporal, which was some scant recognition of the natural discipline of a policeman. A corporal's pay didn't amount to luxury, but he was better off than some of the sturdy lads in whose footsteps he was following. Mary Ellen waited patiently for news of him. He sent field postcards when he could, until, in the following year, he went missing. Mrs Williams looked at her young family now numbering five and there was dread in her heart.

Men left for France and men came back to the Vale. Messages were sent out and brought back. Those who came on leave were sought out by women whose men were away in the hope that confirmation of their wellbeing could be obtained. Mary Ellen asked and asked in vain. The authorities, besieged by hundreds upon hundreds of anxious, waiting women, could give very little reassurance. They had none for Mary Ellen Williams. Corporal Arthur Howell Williams, R.W.F., was missing. There was nothing to add but the words 'believed killed'. The words had been omitted more for clerical reasons than from a compassionate motive. No one knew what had happened to his mangled and shell-battered unit and the men from the Vale. Mrs Williams asked and waited and asked again.

There was at last a day when the sun shone, however. A soldier presented himself at the Police Station door in Tanygrisau.

'Mrs Williams,' he said, his drawn face peering at her as she half-shrunk away, 'I think I've seen your husband, Arthur.'

She clutched the door handle for support.

'Come in!' she said. 'Come in!'

Shyly the soldier entered the room and took off his cap.

'I'm sure it's him,' he said. 'I seen him in a hospital.

He didn't know me when I said, "Hello, Policeman Williams. What you doing here?" but I'm sure it was him! He looked dazed. Shell-shocked, I shouldn't wonder. They moved me on out of there. You should write and ask them to make a search of the records. I've got the name of the hospital on a bit of paper. French name it had.'

She smiled, not at the obviousness of what the man had said, but with the warmth of renewed hope.

'Dazed, but how else was he?' she asked. 'Was he wounded?'

'He was breathing badly. Think he had bronchitis or something like that. He didn't know who I was. I don't think he knew who he was either. I didn't see a name on his bed.'

Mary Ellen made tea and brought out what she had to offer in the way of food. Afterwards her visitor shook her hand and took his leave, pleased to think that what he had told her had lightened her burden. Mary Ellen sat down and wrote to the address she had been given:

'I am seeking information about Corporal Arthur Howell Williams, my husband, whose particulars I enclose. I have not heard from him for a long time (three months) but a soldier who called today says that he saw a man in your hospital about the end of March who answered to my husband's description. He spoke to him, but he thought that he was dazed and did not know who he was.' It was some time before she had a reply. Williams, Arthur Howell, Cpl No. 26274 was alive, though not exactly well. He was suffering from acute shell-shock and was being shipped home for treatment. He would be examined at home in due course.

The examination confirmed what the doctors in France had already decided for themselves, Arthur Howell Williams was unfit to face the rigours of the battle in the mud of France a second time. He was shell-shocked and

his heart was affected by the severe strain he had under-
gone in the fearful days of the 1915-16 winter. A year
later he was discharged from the army. He had served
his king and country for exactly twenty-four months. He
was one of many who received an ornamental scroll on
which Britannia grasped the Union Jack and the world
was informed that Cpl Williams had served with honour
and had been disabled. This meant that he was entitled
to a pension.

Mary Ellen met him at the station of his discharge.
He was still straight-backed, tall and lean but worn and
drawn, as she might have expected. His amnesia had gone.
He knew who he was, and the faces of his wife and children. His eyes filled with tears at the sight of them. He
drew them to him and looked up at the mountains and
thanked God that he was home.

The police station hadn't changed. It was still the same
ageless stone house that it had always been, and Tanygrisau was incapable of being changed, for it, too, was
built of imperishable stone and slate.

'Welcome home, Arthur,' the villagers said, showing
more friendliness towards the returned soldier than they
had shown the policeman who had gone to change his
uniform. Once in his own house the soldier took off his
puttees, his threadbare tunic and cap and eased himself
into bed. He lay listening to the silence, remembering the
endless roar of the guns, the vibration of the earth, the
rending of the darkness by blinding flashes of light, and
after that, the moaning of wounded men, the smell of
blood and death, of disinfectant and chloroform, the
urgent footfalls of medical orderlies and overworked
doctors. In the middle of the night he cried like a child.
He was home, but he was frightened as he had never
been in France.

It was a long time before the horror left him but it did,
slowly, as the weeks stretched into months and 1917 gave

place to the final year of the war. He often sighed for the comrades he had known, the men of the Vale who hadn't come back to plague his policeman's life with their drunk and riotous behaviour, their fighting and fornicating and being alive in the place. Choking for breath on damp days, when the mountains were shrouded in mist, he would look up at the lowering heavens and tell himself that it was nothing. He at least was walking where many a poor fellow would have loved to be. The beat was pleasant in the sunshine when he could look out over the hills. It was a rugged and beautiful landscape, the country to the south-west. It had never been marred as the landscape in France had been ruined, its trees blasted, its rocks and boulders churned through the soil by shell after shell. That was something for which he would always be thankful. As long as he lived he would never forget the horror of shellfire.

In due course, when the time came, he pinned the miniature medal ribbons on his breast and walked smartly into Blaenau to parade for the Chief Constable. The Chief passed along the ranks and spoke to most of the men.

'Williams,' he said, 'I remember you coming for your interview, walking from Llansilin to Dolgellau. How are you? You've come through, anyway. Your wife and family must thank God for that. How many children have you now?'

He told him that a girl, Greta Olive, had been born just at the very beginning of the war and then they had had a boy just before he left for France. They had called him Thomas Allen. Five healthy children. His wife had brought them to see the inspection.

'I miss some faces here today,' said the Chief. 'A lot of your comrades didn't get back.'

It was true. A lot of bereaved parents, wives, daughters, sons, were watching them and perhaps wondering why some had survived and some had not. The Chief passed on and when the parade was over the inspector came to Constable Williams with some news.

'A little moving around is to take place, Williams. It's on the cards you'll go to Penrhyndeudraeth. Tell your missis, just so it doesn't come too much of a shock. You've had your time at Tanygrisau. You can think of being moved soon. The sea air will do you good.'

It was hardly the breeze of the open sea that made Penrhyndeudraeth a resort of tramps. It was true that the cockle-pickers were able to make a living on the sands of the estuary. He told Mary Ellen. She sighed and said she wasn't looking forward to the upheaval. He wasn't exactly excited about it either. In Tanygrisau he moved the tramps on. In Penrhyndeudraeth they couldn't be moved on until they had spent the night in the workhouse and when they moved on more came that very day.

5

Cockles and Muscles

EVIDENCE IN COURT:

'I proceeded to the Workhouse, wearing socks pulled over my boots in order to prevent the accused from hearing my approach. He must have heard me for when I put my hands on the bed he was not in it. He said, "Stay there or I'll blow your head from between your ears!" I followed him, in spite of the warning.'

AT the inspector's suggestion he walked to Penrhyndeudraeth to meet the out-going constable and see the house his family would occupy. It would be little use asking for anything to be done to the house. There was no money for that, but at least he would get the feel of the place and know what the family was coming to. The walk was pleasant. By the time he was into his stride he could have gone on to Criccieth, or across to Talsarnau! The air was full of the scent of spring. Gorse was in bloom. There was woodsmoke on the breeze and the lark was singing. He came up with a tramp who scowled at him in return for his greeting, but that didn't mar the journey. He was used to the hostility of tramps and vagrants. It was mutual when they plagued his life and he was compelled to hound them. Further on he saw two more tramps hanging about at a gateway into a field. One of them removed his clay pipe from his mouth and spat on the ground. There was no mistaking the meaning of it, but he ignored the provocation and went on. Penrhyn-deudraeth basked in the morning sun. He could hear the clamour of gulls away beyond the village. They were feeding on discarded cockles or rubbish tipped on the shore.

'Ah,' said the constable when he knocked at his door. 'Come in, come in!'

He ducked his head and went through the open door to join the other man, whose tunic was undone, as were his bootlaces.

'I'm not on parade yet,' said the untidy constable. 'Been up all night chasing two fellows out of the work-house. They split a man's head with a bottle. I was called and had to go after them. I got neither of them, but I know where they've gone, and I've a messenger on the way down to Tremadoc.'

P.C. Williams sat down and was glad to rest.

'I've heard about the tramps and the cockle-pickers. I'm not looking forward to them.'

'You been in the army,' said the other. 'I was in it too. Well I was sent to the Middle East, see? You heard of Mecca? That's a holy place for the Arabs and that lot. They all look to Mecca and say their prayers. They all try to go there. Well this place is a kind of Mecca. About the middle of the afternoon, wherever they are, all the vagrants for twenty mile around heads this way. They come swarming in and they queue up for the workhouse ticket.'

The implications of this piece of information began to dawn on P.C. Williams. It meant that he would be occupied for a good part of most afternoons checking the circulated information about men wanted for minor and sometimes major crimes in different parts of the country.

'When you get the tramps to bed you can be sure the cockle-pickers have picked a quarrel with somebody, one of their own, or somebody else. They don't care as long as it's a fight. They're all related, so when you go to separate them you got to watch out they don't all pile on top of you. Never wait to draw your staff. Have it in your hand before you start and lay about you without asking questions, for as sure as you try to make inquiry what it's about somebody will have you down and your head split!'

'Is there anything good about Penrhyndeudraeth?' he asked.

'The air is good,' said the other constable, buttoning his tunic and stooping to tie his boots. 'The weather is good, sometimes. Watch the well, though. That's not good. Boil the water in the summer or you'll never be out of the *ty bach*.'

Before he left he was shown over the house and the garden, inspected the Occurrence Book and admired the way the entries had been made. Some old constables made entries in a wonderful copperplate style, and, it seemed, must have spent more time writing than they had done chasing the offenders whose misdeeds they had recorded: 'It was reported to me that John Jones was causing a disturbance in his father-in-law's house and would not leave. I went to Cemlyn Place and saw John Jones. He had his mother-in-law by the throat and was punching her head. His father-in-law, Elias Roberts, was lying in a corner. I arrested him. . .' The Occurrence Book had plenty to say about John Jones, the most violent of the cockle-pickers. Again and again he was charged with assault, fined ten shillings, one pound, two pounds, served a sentence of seven, fourteen and twenty-one days. But John Jones was only one of many.

'I sometimes spend half a day just getting the book up to date,' said the sleepy constable as P.C. Williams thumbed it over. 'You'll see a John Jones in there.

Watch out for him when you come. He's given me more cramp from writing in that book than anybody else!'

On his way back to Tanygrisau P.C. Williams couldn't help but feel depressed, but by the time he got home he knew he must appear light-hearted for Mary Ellen's sake. She wouldn't relish taking the children to a place he painted as a haunt of delinquents, cockle-picking wild men and violent tramps who almost murdered one another with bottles.

'Well then?' said Mary Ellen as she put his tea before him. 'Did you like what you saw?'

'Beautiful sunshine,' he said, 'birds singing. You could smell the sea in the air.'

He didn't say that what was in the air was not the sea but the odour of abandoned cockle gatherings, even although there was still an 'r' in the month.

'It sounds not so bad then. Is the house all right?'

He told her about the house and the damp patches on walls and ceilings. It wasn't the house that would shock her quite so much as the influx of workhouse characters, in their rags and tatters, carrying their bundles and smoke-blackened tin cans and looking about to see what they could steal.

'It's not like Tanygrisau,' he felt compelled to say. 'More life, more coming and going. The chap there said it was like a place in the Middle East, really—Mecca.'

'That seems strange,' said Mary Ellen. 'How can any-where in Wales be like the Middle East? Are there Arabs there then?'

He realized how near he had come to making a mistake. 'No,' he lied. 'No, not Arabs, just people. What the chap meant was that it had the same look as a holy place.'

Having said as much he thought it timely to choke on his bread and butter and make a fuss coughing. The less Mary Ellen was told about Penrhyndeudraeth until she got there, the better! Already she had remarked about the workhouse. If she thought very long, even the word Mecca might begin to create a different impression in her mind.

A fortnight later they were removed to Penrhyndeudraeth. The police station had the same damp smell as the one they had left. It was scrubbed and cleaned. On the table lay the Occurrence Book and a fat file of official circulars bearing photographs of wanted men and their descriptions—colour of hair, height, weight, colour of eyes and other characteristics. The crimes listed ranged from petty larceny to rape and murder. Some of these men might pass through the workhouse. The new constable's duty was to make himself as familiar as possible with the faces of wanted men thought to be in the area, or likely to move into it. The workhouse was Mecca. It was also a good hiding place for men on the run.

The first Sunday he was stationed in Penrhyndeudraeth P.C. Williams was doing his best to arrange the furniture when there was a knock at the door.

'Are you there, policeman?' an anxious voice inquired.

He put down his corner of the settee and answered the door.

'You better come. John Jones is at it again!'

John Jones was at it to much better effect than the singers in the chapel. While they could be heard halfway down the street he could be heard in every corner of the place! P.C. Williams remembered the advice of the man who had held office in the village before. He slipped into his tunic and took firm hold not of his staff, but of a hefty walking stick.

'John Jones will have to be accommodated,' he told Mary Ellen. 'The better the day, the better the deed. If I don't come back I'll get a police funeral, teh?'

Mary Ellen watched him striding down the street. He wasn't exactly running, but anyone who saw him could hardly mistake his determination and courage.

The affray, for it was more than a one-man disturbance, the John Jones faction having confronted the Roberts family, was in a healthy state by the time the constable arrived on the scene.

'All right!' he said, wading in. 'Have done!'

He gave the nearest battler a hearty rap with his walking stick, striking him on the shoulder and rendering his right arm useless. His immediate opponent was served in the same manner. A third man was bundled back into a flower bed. The impression the policeman was making would soon have brought order to the scene had not someone hit him with a stone, knocking his helmet off. The two families, well aware that charges would involve both sides, did everything they could to put the policeman out of action so that they could make themselves scarce, but P.C. Williams, even with his heart in his mouth, grabbed John Jones and began to heave him along out of the garden in which the battle had been mainly conducted. Blows fell upon him but he held on, foiling a rescue operation with wild sweeping strokes of his walking stick while the fingers of one hand remained hooked into the collar of both the jacket and shirt of the man he was determined to take in.

'Let go of him!' screamed John Jones's wife, rushing forward with a cooking pot in her hand. The stick struck the pot and the pot sailed away to fall in the road where it shattered in black iron fragments.

'Resisting arrest,' P.C. Williams said through his teeth.

John Jones said nothing that might have been repeated to the magistrates. All four-letter words were written down and handed up on a piece of paper, but P.C. Williams could hardly have remembered all the words the cockle-picker used.

'I think you'd better hold the door for me, Mary Ellen,' he suggested when at last he brought the struggling man to the front of the police station, 'because he doesn't seem to want to come in.'

Mary Ellen held the door. John Jones braced his feet against the steps and then against the doorpost. P.C. Williams discouraged him with hard raps on the knees and at last the prisoner was brought in and the handcuffs put on him.

The windows of the room were small-paned and the woodwork was supplemented by iron bars. At different times it had been found necessary to repair windows and make the room into a more substantial lock-up than it had been. P.C. Williams looked round and made sure that his prisoner couldn't get out or inflict damage upon himself or anything of value in the room.

'My advice to you, my lad,' he said, 'is to sit here quietly until you sober up. I'll have your statement if you've got anything to say when I've had my dinner. After that we'll see about a trip to Blaenau where they'll make you more comfortable, teh?'

John Jones said nothing. Mary Ellen looked anxiously at her husband. There was a lot of noise outside. The cockle-pickers evidently expected to prise John Jones free of the policeman's hand.

'This is a fine start,' said Mary Ellen. 'The children all terrified and a crowd outside.'

'Don't you worry about that,' said her husband. 'I'll have them all inside if they don't clear off. I start as I mean to go on!'

He went out to the door and this time he had his truncheon in his hand.

'Look,' he said, raising his voice above the clamour of the Jones tribe. 'I haven't been here long enough to get my furniture straight yet. We haven't much room in there, so if I take any of you in you'll have to be laid flat. I reckon I can take a dozen. I'll take anybody that stays here another minute. I'll charge them with creating a disturbance. When I've counted five I'm hauling you in!'

Someone at the back threw a stone. He didn't hesitate but charged forward and swung his truncheon, striking out right and left until he had the offender. The man who had thrown the stone had a knife in his hand by this time. The truncheon almost broke the hand that held the knife, but P.C. Williams took time to pick up the weapon and bring it along with his second prisoner into the police station.

'Two, three . . .' he shouted as he bundled the owner of the knife through the door.

The crowd began to retreat. P.C. Williams found a second pair of handcuffs which his predecessor had left behind and secured the second prisoner with them. When he reached the door he counted four and five. There was no one within earshot. The Jones tribe had retreated down the road.

'I'll have my dinner now,' he told white-faced Mary Ellen. 'Don't worry any more. Let's have something to eat. I got to think what the charges might be.'

Mary Ellen and the children sat down at the table a little apprehensively for the two prisoners were cursing merrily and making as much disturbance as they could.

'Next Sunday,' said Arthur Williams, the family man, 'we maybe get some peace and go to a church service?'

Mary Ellen nodded. After a minute he got up and went through to the locked room. There was silence when he came back.

'Well?' said Mary Ellen.

He looked steadily at her. 'They were assaulting each other with their feet. I had to restrain one of them. The other one decided to keep still. I don't blame him. He's had a lively morning.'

A wonderful peace seemed to settle over the place after that as the family supped their soup and had their first Sunday dinner in Penrhyndeudraeth.

The sergeant and inspector were grim when they considered the report. It was one thing to make an arrest and haul in a well-known delinquent but it was another to get the necessary evidence to make the charge stick. The charge was read to John Jones: '. . . that you did on April 30th resist one P.C. Williams No. 21, a constable of the Merioneth Constabulary whilst in the execution of his duty . . . Prevention of Crimes Act 1871 . . . and to Mervyn Jones . . . resist one P.C. Williams . . .' All at once P.C. Williams saw what keeping the peace among the cockle-pickers meant. It didn't mean copperplate writing in the Occurrence Book, and charges. It meant something very different. It meant rough and ready justice on the spot. It meant being the head man in the place so that simply walking down the street would be enough to make the worst terror think twice and then take to his heels. If a cockle knife was pulled out of a man's pocket he had to be whacked so hard that he couldn't use his hand to open a cockle for a month and the sergeant and inspector from Blaenau, when they came down had nothing to do but admire the sunlight on the backs of the gulls far away, almost at Harlech!

'Do you know what that lot on Sunday comes to?' he asked Mary Ellen. 'Resisting arrest, drunk and riotous, that's the best they can make of it. The windows they broke were broken by persons unknown, of course. All right, I've got to go down the road and encourage one of them and when he tries it on I've got to hammer him!'

This wasn't really something he hadn't known before, of course, for he had occasionally had to restrain a pugnacious customer or take his stick to a boy stealing apples from a garden. The law was the law, but justice could be instant, without a working man getting a record or a boy having a blot on his character. Many a lad who had taken his medicine in the old-fashioned way grew up to become not only a respectable citizen but a pillar of society. The cockle-pickers might not undergo such a radical change of character, but they would take justice on the spot in future! It was too far to haul them all to Blaenau, and further still to Caernarvon where the jail was and criminal cases were tried.

A week after he had been fined John Jones saw fit to settle accounts with the new constable. They met in the street when one had taken his quota of ale and the other was hungry for his supper. A hungry man is sometimes quickly fatigued, but he fights hard.

'Come out and see John Jones giving it to the new policeman!' they said. The news ran up and down the street. Not everyone rushed out at once but it was barely five minutes before the message had changed. 'Come and see the new policeman giving it to John Jones! Like a board, he is, like a tough old fence post, like he was made of iron.'

They battled in the middle of the road and no one went to the assistance of John Jones. Mary Ellen heard the news and shut the children in the house. She was half-inclined to lend her husband a hand, but dared not. He wasn't going to have it said that he had needed help and in fact he needed none. His long, lean body reached out and his hard bony arms were like the shafts of quarry hammers. He was wearing his tunic but his helmet which had fallen, was cradled in the arms of a small, ragged boy. John Jones had finally received justice. He was brought round with a jug of water from the well and never again would he ignore the village policeman's command. The village took note. The cockle-pickers would fight again, but never when P.C. Williams was about, and never when he ordered them to stop. In time John Jones forgot his humiliation and would stop to pass the time of day with the policeman. They even got to discussing the question of behaviour and keeping the peace.

'Rely on me, John Jones,' said the policeman. 'I won't

run you in. You behave yourself and I won't lift a finger.'

There was nothing else that really needed to be said. The cockle-pickers lived by the rule that a man who could hammer his point home was respected. A score of fines and spells in prison was water off the duck's back.

While this applied with the cockle-pickers there was no lesson that could be taught the men and women who were itinerants and appeared like a plague of locusts. P.C. Williams chased them for stealing a loaf, a chicken from the backyard, clothes from the clothes-line, money from a child, and they swarmed through one another until he hardly knew who was who. The man with the tattoo on his wrists was a different matter. The day he came for inspection P.C. Williams was busy. All he noticed was the letter 'S' on the lower part of the man's left wrist, but that evening, turning over his sheets he saw reference to Soldier Sims, wanted for housebreaking in a dozen places, a violent man known to carry firearms. He sometimes travelled about from one workhouse or Union to the next, particularly after committing offences and spending the money.

'Look, Mary Ellen,' he said, 'I got this fellow in my area. He came this afternoon. He's in the Union now. I saw the letter 'S' on his left wrist. I didn't see his right arm, but he answers the description. I bet he has the same on his right wrist. He carries firearms and shouldn't be rushed for he's been known to use a gun to escape.'

'What do you do then?' asked Mary Ellen, her face showing her anxiety.

'I go and see Old Morrison and get him to find out what bed this Soldier Sims is lying on. I go in in the middle of the night and I try to get him before he knows anything about it.'

It sounded simple. It didn't sound so simple when the

workhouse master pointed out that although there was no
light in the long room in which the inmates slept, some
of them sat talking all night. They weren't like ordinary
working men. Some of them lay sleeping in the sun all
day and only came in for companionship at night. Some
of them brought little tots of spirits with them and handed
their drink round in the dark. It wouldn't be easy to steal
up on the wanted man even if he happened to be asleep,
for someone would warn him. The workhouse population
had no reason to co-operate with the police. On the
contrary, they made it a point of honour to frustrate the
police wherever and whenever they could.

'If he has a gun,' said the workhouse master, 'you
might get it while he is doing his task before he goes in
the morning.'

The policeman didn't like that. A criminal of Sims's
sort was bound to keep his gun close at hand. He must
be taken while asleep.

'I might put something in his drink,' said the workhouse master, but without much enthusiasm.

'No,' said the policeman. 'I'll sit up until after three
then I'm coming in to get him. I'll put some old socks
over my boots. I'll have my staff. I'll be there before he
can get the gun out.'

Mary Ellen listened with growing apprehension.

'You should send for help or let him go somewhere
else and be caught,' she said.

The thought had never entered her husband's head.
He smiled at her and rubbed his chin.

'I'm the policeman here,' he said. 'He's wanted and
he's here. I got my duty to do, haven't I?'

It was a dreary vigil, sitting in the house waiting for
three o'clock to chime. In preparation for the event P.C.
Williams had pulled old socks over his boots. He was
ready and keyed up for the encounter. The clock ticking
did nothing to reduce the tension and at last just before

the hour chimed he let himself out of the house. Mary Ellen got out of bed and watched him go, but the five children slept soundly.

The workhouse brooded. An owl perched on its roof but it sat without calling. Far away over the estuary seabirds were crying as they always did. In the scrub trees to the south-east a dog barked. The policeman walked the dry road like a ghost. Penrhyndeudraeth was in shadow but dawn was little more than an hour away. There was no one at the door to greet him. He turned the handle and found it open, as Old Morrison had promised. The time had come! He took two or three steps along the corridor and paused to listen. It seemed that someone was talking, but he couldn't be sure that it wasn't some poor devil rambling in his sleep. Another step and then another. Something, perhaps a rat, scuttled along the stone floor at a great rate, but that was all. He slipped through the half-open door and stood at the end of the room counting the windows so that he could be sure where Sims lay. Gingerly he paced the space between the iron beds and at last he stood where he judged the criminal lay. He reached out and gently felt across the bed. There was nothing there. The bed had been vacated. Sims had gone! He reached out and felt across the bed from bottom to top and then straightened.

"All right, Mr Policeman!' said a gruff voice. 'Just stay there or I'll blow your head out from between your ears!'

He stood very still. Although it was as black as in the cupboard below the stairs, he began to see outlines. Soldier Sims was on his way up the aisle between the beds. He was off! With great determination P.C. Williams forced himself to take step for step with him. At the doorway Sims paused. The frame of the door revealed him there with a bundle hanging from one hand. The other hand was in shadow but the policeman didn't need to be told what it held or where the gun was pointing. He stood still and Sims stood still.

'Go back, you bastard!' said Soldier Sims.

He made no reply. He hadn't said a word since he had left the police station. His throat and tongue were dry. He had never been more frightened, even in France. All at once the door flapped shut. Sims was out and down the corridor. Perhaps he was standing at the main door, waiting for him. He followed, nevertheless, knowing that he was going to lose any chance of arresting the criminal if he stayed where he was a moment longer. Sims had gone out on to the road, for he wasn't there in the corridor. Grasping his staff, P.C. Williams ran the length of the corridor and bounded out of the door. Sims was on the road, a grey figure, hesitating, with the bundle now slung on his shoulder and the gun in his hand.

'I told you!' he said.

The roar of the gun awakened the village. Mary Ellen sprang to the door in her nightdress, frightened almost out of her wits. In the cottages of the village people turned over and sat up. What in the name of God had happened? The workhouse master, Old Morrison, struggled into his trousers. Murder had been done, he told himself. The policeman had paid the price for trying to catch a criminal with a gun. So it might have been, but Soldier Sims had never been in the army and his marksmanship was below average. The bullet from his gun lodged in the stonework of a near-by cottage. His second shot was a misfire. His ammunition was bad, but the policeman's aim was sure. The whirling staff, flying like a boomerang, struck its target. Sims crashed to the ground, dazed and fumbling for the gun he had dropped. A moment later P.C. Williams was helping him to his feet. It was done! The business of handcuffing was one in which he had had some training and experience. Soldier Sims was quickly under control, cursing his rotten luck.

'Bad luck,' agreed his captor. 'But if I hadn't got you the hangman would have had you in the end, stretched and dangling?'

The gun was safely in his tunic pocket and Sims was on his way to the police station before the first sleepy villager was on the road asking Old Morrison whatever had happened.

'I don't know for sure, but Williams came in the night to arrest a man with a gun. He's got him, fair play to him, though if you ask me he should be locked up himself, considering he's got a wife and five children to think about.'

This time the charge was one the inspector didn't have to scratch his head over. Sims was hauled off for trial at Caernarvon. P.C. Williams's conduct was commended by the Chief Constable. The village looked upon him with even greater respect than before. He wasn't large and fat, like the old sergeant, nor as imposing and dignified as the Chief Constable when he happened to make a visit in the area. He didn't have the presence of the Superintendent who jogged in on his horse and called for oats for it while he stayed overnight to check the books, but he was a formidable fellow, as hard as the hardest of them, and quite without fear. Does his duty, they said. You got to give him that. No trouble here but he can handle it. Even the tramps get over his boundary before they set on one another.

'Mecca,' he said. 'They all make a pilgrimage to Mecca! I wait here for them and they come to me, driven by all the constables for miles, hurrying like rats at threshing time. I could fill the book with cases.'

'I remember you telling me that it was a sort of holy place,' said Mary Ellen accusingly. 'I remember, and I don't forgive you!'

He had to smile as he plodded off to chivvy his daily quota of vagrants on their way. Some were comparatively harmless characters like the wandering blacksmith and the tinker who tried to scrape a few shillings together and achieve something better than a bed in the workhouse. Some were on an endless circular tour, appearing in the same week of the same month, month after month or year after year. The thieves had their pattern of thieving, this one robbing hen runs, that one stealing from village shops, this one pretending to sell something at the front of the house while his companion stole at the back door. It was an offence to be without money, an offence to strike the workhouse master, to fail to complete the daily task, or to abscond. It was also an offence to sleep out-of-doors, to light a fire by the side of the road, or to beg. The sleepers-out had to be checked at farm barns and outhouses, sheds and old haystacks. The thieves searched and charged.

'The smell of them turns me up,' said P.C. Williams. 'But the sight of them would break your heart. I've seen men in worse condition in France, but not much worse, no lousier, no dirtier, no hungrier. If they move me I hope it'll be a long way away from this place. It may have a touch of sea air when the wind blows from the estuary, but when it doesn't I swear I can smell the tramps on their way in.'

Mary Ellen, too, prayed that they would soon move to a place where there was less trouble and fewer tramps. The inspector said that a move might not be too long coming. How would she like Trawsfynydd? There was a nice clean little place, in the middle of nowhere, and the sun shone on it.

6

The Lilies of the Field

EVIDENCE IN COURT:
'She told me, The baby cried and wouldn't stop. I hit it with a stone that came in my hand. It wasn't murder. I didn't murder her. I loved her!'

Two pieces of information arrived by bus while P.C. Williams was at the side of the house pumping up the tyres of the new bicycle to make sure they were just right. The first was the most important. He stuck the bicycle pump into his trouser pocket and called Mary Ellen.

'It's Trawsfynydd on the twenty-eighth,' he said. 'You can start sorting things out.'

They were going and that was that, but the second piece of news produced a similar slight anxiety even although it was routine. It concerned a woman named Lily Maggs, Lily the Brass, some called her. She was wanted in half a dozen places for soliciting for prostitution, taking the wallets of amorous farmers, or their turnip-like gold watches if she could lay her hands on nothing more valuable while her customers were concentrating on other matters. Nowhere was she wanted more than in the county of Caernarvon, where she had shuttled to and fro from market to market, earning her living in the oldest profession in the world. She was thought to be on her way from Caernarvon through Portmadoc to Dolgellau. The Caernarvonshire police were hot on her trail, but the real significance of the travels of Lily Maggs wasn't how she might corrupt the easily corruptible, but the tally on the books at Caernarvon or Dolgellau when H.M. Inspector of Constabulary made his visit. The score was important. The 'big man' would run his finger down the record and make comparison. Here was a case that might be marked down to Merioneth or go to the credit of Caernarvon. Lily Maggs, if she travelled along the coast, would head for the cob at Portmadoc, and the cob, short-cutting the estuary inlet, was already the scene of many a tussle with thieves, beggars and others striving to escape the clutches of members of one or the other of the two Police Forces.

'Think about it,' he said. 'I've got to be on my way to the cob. A woman we want is heading this way. I'll hide by the wall and see if I can nail her. The Chief will be pleased if we catch what slips through their fingers in Portmadoc!'

Mary Ellen watched him ride off on the shining new bicycle, riding bolt upright and looking very smart. She hoped he would be home in time for his lunch, but she knew he might be away until dark, for the watch on the cob was a serious thing on occasions of this sort.

On his way to the cob he met one of the cockle-pickers returning from selling his wares in Portmadoc. They stopped to talk for a few minutes.

'I don't suppose you saw a yellow-haired woman, five foot three, well built, heavily made-up, named Lily Maggs?' asked the policeman.

The cockle-picker leered at him. 'Seen her? I was with her an hour ago! A right bit she is! Took me half-crown and wanted another. After she was gone I found she'd dipped me pocket and took five shilling more!'

'Where was she?'

'Where was she wasn't my luck to find out! Gone!'

Hurriedly the policeman remounted his bicycle. Lily Maggs was at Portmadoc, anyhow. The chances were that the police there now had news of her. She would be on her way over the cob! He began to ride as fast as he could. He was less than half a mile from the long, straight causeway across the water when he saw a woman coming his way. She was short, fair-haired and walked with a swagger. Lily Maggs, a lily of the field who toiled not! The sermon on Sunday had been on that very subject. Now here was the wanted woman hurrying right into his arms and Caernarvon was out of luck, or almost out of luck.

Lily the Brass wasn't short-sighted. She quickly saw her danger and whirled about and began to head for the cob, her skirts dragged up to her hips so that she could run the faster. P.C. Williams found himself puffing as he pedalled for all he was worth. Lily wasn't going to escape across the cob! What was almost worse than her escaping was the fact that the Portmadoc representative of law and order was on his way down the cob, and he too, was riding for all he was worth. They were on a collision course, it seemed, and Lily Maggs was the prize.

Both bicycles reached the scuttling woman at the same moment and each was thrown on the ground and lay there with wheels whirling. Each constable grabbed the absconding prostitute and began tugging at her arms. She was dragged a foot or so towards Caernarvon's territory, and then back a foot or two deeper into Merioneth. It was a tug of war.

'She's mine, Williams!' cursed the constable from Portmadoc. 'Let her go, or I'll take you both into Portmadoc!'

Arthur Howell Williams was as determined a policeman as had ever laid hands on a prisoner. He wasn't going to give up now. He pushed his rival with all his strength. The Portmadoc man stumbled and fell! Now things had gone a little too far. P.C. Williams could only apologize and help the other man to his feet.

'Give up!' he said. 'She was on my side. I caught her on my side even if you got your hands on her. Now come on, be reasonable!'

The Portmadoc constable scowled and allowed himself to be helped.

'Beggar off, Williams!' he said. 'I'll see you in hell first! She's mine!'

At that moment Lily Maggs solved the problem by jumping over the wall into the water. She was more than able to look after herself in the water. She swam away, her clothes billowing round her ample legs as she struck out for the far side, the marsh on the Penrhyndeudraeth boundary.

'Whatever you like to say now,' said the Merioneth constable, 'she's made her choice. She's on my side. I'll arrest her. Your lot can file charges, but we do the arresting?'

He didn't wait to hear what the Portmadoc man had to say, but jumped on his bicycle and rode to a place where he knew Lily Maggs would return to the road. In half an hour she obliged, wading out of the marshy field on to the road right in front of him.

'Sod!' she yelled. 'You threw me in the water!'

He was well-used to wild accusations.

'Come with me,' he said. 'My missis will get your clothes dried out. We maybe even got something for you to eat.'

Lily Maggs was resigned to her fate, but she didn't respond to kindness. She cursed him.

'Whether my parents were married or not isn't going to do you much good, Lily,' he said. 'I don't suppose your father stayed long enough to leave his name!'

They went on into Penrhyndeudraeth in silence, Lily's

saturated clothing leaving a water trail on the dry road. A procession of ragged children accompanied them to the police station. They formed a crowd outside while Mrs Williams took the wet clothing of the cursing prostitute and hung it round the fire. Lily Maggs was completely unconcerned when some of the bolder children peered in at the windows. P.C. Williams had to drive them away.

'They seen it before!' she cackled when the policeman drew the curtains.

She was a hard case. The trade she had followed hadn't done much to improve her.

'When the inspector gets here,' he told her, 'and I'm sending for him right away, you'll be dealt with for whatever offences they have down against you in Merioneth. After that Caernarvon can have you, I shouldn't wonder.'

The inspector came late in the afternoon. He rubbed his hands with delight. 'You chalked one up there, Williams,' he said. 'She can go to Caernarvon tomorrow. Your missis can take her in the morning, and you get her signed for!'

The instruction meant that Lily Maggs, duly charged, was to stay the night at Penrhyndeudraeth in the custody of P.C. and Mrs Williams, acting police matron. The next day she would be conveyed by train through Portmadoc to Caernarvon.

In the morning they gave their prisoner breakfast and saw that she had no excuse for making them late for the train. A crowd followed them down to the little railway station and crowded on to the platform to see them off. Lily Maggs cursed the policeman and his wife.

'You know what he tried to do last night?' she shouted. 'Tried to sleep with me! Dirty sod!'

Mary Ellen flushed. Her husband frowned and ordered the prostitute to keep her tongue between her teeth, or she would find herself facing extra charges. Lily Maggs was not daunted. When the train came she was still using foul language and complaining that her virtue was threatened at every turn. In the compartment into which she was bundled she indulged in another and more embarrassing display. She hauled up her dress and showed her thighs. She made indecent suggestions to the two men on the opposite seat and told them how intimately the policeman had searched her person. Mary Ellen looked out of the window, becoming red-faced and more uncomfortable as the journey proceeded. At Portmadoc and then on the dreary, wind-blown platform at Afonwen, where they changed trains, Lily Maggs advertised her plight to the world, using words that made those who heard them look upward towards heaven.

'Like to love me for half-a-crown?' she demanded of the first man they encountered in Caernarvon. 'You can, if they'll give us five minutes!'

Mary Ellen hauled her along. P.C. Williams dearly wished he could silence the prostitute with his staff. He had had more than enough and he knew how deeply poor Mary Ellen was shamed. At the prison they signed her in and took the receipt testifying to the delivery of 'the body of one, Lily Marie Maggs, common prostitute, arrested for soliciting, picking pockets, etc., etc.'

P.C. Williams, making his signature in the official record sighed:

'You could add, using insulting language, indecency and two or three more. You're welcome to her.'

Mary Ellen said nothing until they were in the train on their way back to the junction at Afonwen.

'I had heard about that kind of woman,' she said, 'but I never came across one in my life before. I hope I never do again.'

She had spoken a little prematurely. They hadn't finished with women of the oldest profession. There was another Lily dogging their footsteps, a friend of Lily

Maggs, albeit a mere beginner at the trade. She they would meet at Trawsfynydd in less than a month.

The Occurrence Book was duly made up before P.C. Williams took his leave of Penrhyndeudraeth and the cockle-pickers. Against the case of Lily Maggs the outgoing policeman's successor would enter the punishment given out by the magistrates when, in due course, she answered the charges.

It was on the day that the Williams family moved to Trawsfynydd that Old Morrison, master of the workhouse, counted his blankets and found one missing. He hesitated and decided not to make a complaint. The blanket wasn't exactly new. The woman who had taken it had had a child in her arms. Old Morrison, hard though he was, hadn't the heart to see her punished, for she had been not just young but gaunt and miserable.

Trawsfynydd stands on a little hill. Its street winds over the rise. It begins and it ends with nothing more striking than the typical stone, slated cottages of a thousand other little Welsh hamlets. Here, in the middle of nowhere, P.C. Williams set himself down to follow his calling and serve the Constabulary once again. He liked the compactness of the little place and the breadth of the landscape beyond. Sometimes he looked at the hills and the moorland between and was thankful that Manchester had pained him so acutely. Whatever life might be like in the backwaters of the villages it was a thousand times more endurable than it would have been in places like Salford. Nothing happened in Trawsfynydd, they said, and very little in the space between this settlement and neighbouring places. Tramps came through and found nothing to stay for. Irish labourers sometimes came in from work schemes in the surrounding country and drank and argued a little more than they should have done. They gave their names and were charged in due course, Tom Reilly, Sean Kelly, Daniel Flynn, Duffy, Maldoon and O'Brien, drunk

and riotous, causing a disturbance on licensed premises
and fighting in the street. He rattled their heads together
or talked to them and persuaded them to go and lie in
the outhouse until they were sober. They were harmless,
or nearly harmless. Crime was something Trawsfynydd
didn't really know, or hadn't known until a bright morning when P.C. Williams found himself with murder on
his hands.

'Speak slowly,' he said. 'Tell me over again, and take
your time. Where were you? What did you see and what
time was it?'

'I was going down the stream,' said his informant,
'looking for a place where I might catch a fish, and there,
in the pool beside the little bridge, I found it, a child,
dead. It would be about half an hour ago.'

There was a proper procedure to be observed. Name
and address of the person giving the information, the time
and the place of the alleged incident, the facts so that they
were on record, and then investigation of the alleged
offence, if offence there had been.

'Very well then, Jones Papershop, we'll go and take a
look. You touched nothing? You told nobody else?'

The witness testified that he had mentioned not a word
to a soul. He had touched nothing. He was also quite
sober and in his right mind. A child had been thrown into
the water, it was dead. It had been murdered!

P.C. Williams said nothing to this last piece of evidence.
He had been schooled in discretion. What a witness saw
and what he thought he saw were generally very different
things. Imagination was not a great asset in the initial
stages. The 'murdered baby' might turn out to be a
discarded doll. They walked down out of the village and
along the road to the bridge over the stream. P.C.
Williams made his guide stay there on the bridge and
clambered down to get into the water so that he could
reach the bundle in the pool without disturbing anything

on the bank. There was no mistake. A child had been
killed, not just dropped into the stream, or left there after
it had died, but killed with a stone! At least one stone
was embedded in the skull of the infant which lay in the
blanket. P.C. Williams looked at it and his heart was
heavy. For a moment he forgot that he was a policeman
with a job to do. He thought of his own children, of a
child as yet to be born, and the effect of the tragedy upon
his own wife and family.

He climbed back up out of the stream by the bridge.

'Stay here, Jones,' he said. 'Don't let anybody go down
there. Nothing must be touched. I've got to report this.'

Mary Ellen listened to what he told her. She was filled
with horror.

'Who can have done it?' she asked.

He shrugged his shoulders. 'If I knew that I'd have
them locked up, but I don't. Some heartless, mad creature
did it, but it's nobody from here. I could count the
children on two hands. I know everybody already, so it
must be somebody passing through, some gipsy maybe,
some tinker's woman. It was killed with a stone, bashed
on the head. There was a stone bedded in its skull. It
lay there in a dirty blanket with red stitching on it. The
blanket might tell us something, but we'll have to wait.'

'Can I go and look?' asked Mary Ellen.

'Nobody goes there until the inspector and the rest get
here,' he said. 'There may be evidence about.'

Down by the bridge a crowd had somehow materialized
and its numbers increased during the afternoon until,
when the inspector arrived, the road was blocked.

P.C. Williams stepped forward and saluted.

'I have left things just as they were, sir,' he said. 'I
couldn't stop the crowd gathering. It was hard enough
stopping boys working their way down the stream.'

The inspector nodded and went scrambling down to
the pool where the body lay, half-wrapped in the grey

blanket. He instructed P.C. Williams to look out for the doctor, who had been summoned earlier, and knelt down to examine the blanket and its contents.

'Might be an army blanket,' he said.

He couldn't think of any other angle. After a minute or two he bent over and scooped up the pathetic bundle and brought it up to the side of the bridge.

'It was thrown down there, Williams,' he said. 'Thrown from the bank, or even the bridge. It was dead before it was thrown.'

P.C. Williams said nothing. He followed the inspector up the road after posting a man to see that no one approached the bank of the stream. The man he had chosen farmed the land on either side. He was filled with self-importance. No one would be allowed anywhere near the place, he said. The police could be sure of that! Few remained by the bridge at all, however, and the little farmer was left to keep himself company and brandish his stick at the small boys who occasionally tried to go over the wall. The village followed the inspector and his burden all the way to the police station. At the door the inspector paused, jerked his head and ordered P.C. Williams to send the spectators about their business. P.C. Williams sighed and looked at them.

'Go on home,' he said. 'You'll see nothing here. You'll learn more at home than you will standing in the road.'

They retreated a short distance. He went into the office and closed the door, opening it again to admit the doctor who had come by pony and trap and left the pony hitched to the railing.

'A female child,' said the doctor. 'Ill-nourished. About ten weeks old. Killed by having its skull crushed by a stone. Not an accident. Dead about eight or ten hours. Check the registers, if I were you.'

'Whoever killed it took away whatever clothes it had,' said the inspector. 'And left this old army blanket.'

At that moment Mary Ellen knocked on the door.

'Would you like a cup of tea, Inspector?' she asked.

The inspector looked at her and quickly turned the blanket to cover the gory sight of the murdered child. He didn't need to be told that the constable's wife was expecting another baby. He was an old-fashioned fellow and believed that such a sight might result in the unborn child being born disfigured or malformed.

'Thank you very much indeed, Mrs Williams. Don't come in with it. Stay out of here, for pity's sake! Let Arthur bring the tea when you've made it.'

Mary Ellen closed the door. She had made the tea and was about to knock again when her husband came through for it.

'Arthur,' she said, 'you get on your bicycle and hurry to Penrhyndeudraeth. That blanket came from there!'

The constable in Arthur Williams made him hesitate before accepting anything anyone said, or urged him to do. He was by nature a cautious fellow.

'Hold on,' he said. 'Hold on. I can't just do that! It might not be a workhouse blanket.'

'Even if it isn't a workhouse blanket,' said Mary Ellen, her mouth set grimly, 'I know it came from the workhouse because I take notice of stitching. I saw that blanket there when I was last in the Union. I tell you I know it is from there. So go you to Penrhyndeudraeth and ask who took it away. You'll find it was whoever murdered that child!'

Arthur took the tea and sidled through the door to put it on the corner of the table. The inspector and the doctor helped themselves.

'Sir,' said Arthur, apprehensively, 'I have something to say. My wife was a dressmaker, a needlewoman by trade. She only got a glimpse of this blanket, but she knows it's a blanket she saw at the workhouse. She is telling me to get on my bicycle and ride to Penrhyn and ask who stole it.'

'She is, is she?' said the inspector. 'I'll have to talk to her then!'

He stood up and went through to speak to Mary Ellen.

'Mrs Williams,' he said, 'I don't like anybody doing my job for me but you seem to think you have a talent for catching murderers! You sure about what you say?'

Mary Ellen drew herself up. 'Mr Inspector,' she said, 'you sign your name with a pen. You sign your name with a needle! I know! That blanket is from Penrhyndeudraeth. Go there and ask them. You'll be on the track of whoever took it, and whoever killed the baby!'

'I think you're right, Mrs Williams. You better take charge of things while we're gone. Williams and I will go and look into this.'

P.C. Williams sighed when the inspector told him. Mary Ellen was getting altogether too bossy. He followed the inspector out and together they prepared to go to Penrhyndeudraeth on bicycles. But the doctor, who had been adjusting the harness on his pony, came over and offered to convey them to the workhouse himself and in a short time they were jogging along the quiet road to that place.

'It was a young woman called Lily Conroy,' said Old Morrison when he looked at the blanket they had brought. 'That is our blanket and she took it. What's happened?'

'Murder has happened,' said the inspector. 'Do you know where Lily Conroy went?'

'I don't know,' said the old fellow. 'I expect she went on to Dolgellau. She was a prostitute, a crony of the woman you arrested a little while ago, Lily Maggs.'

'The lilies of the field,' said P.C. Williams.

'We've got one. We've got to get the other,' said the inspector. 'Mrs Williams'll make a policeman of you yet!'

Arthur smiled. They left the workhouse master, warning

him that a statement would be required quite soon.
The doctor was waiting to take them back to Trawsfynydd.

They arrived at the police station to discover that the
crowd had reassembled and P.C. Williams was once again
ordered to make them disperse.

'What's happening, Williams?' one of them asked.

'We have some information,' he said. 'We're looking
for a young woman from the workhouse, red-haired, thin,
about eighteen years old, wearing a green dress and shoes
that are loose on her feet.'

He felt justified in imparting this much to the village
gossip. For all he and the inspector knew, the young
woman might be still in the locality.

'You were right, Mary Ellen,' he said. 'We checked
with Old Morrison. It was one of his blankets. It was
stolen by a young woman called Lily Conroy, a friend of
that woman we took to Caernarvon!'

'I told you so,' said Mary Ellen. 'She was wearing a
green dress?'

It was all as much as P.C. Williams could take. 'Hold
on,' he said, 'you know too much!'

'I saw her this morning,' said Mary Ellen. 'She was
picking flowers in that field down there.'

'Inspector,' he said, hurrying into the office. 'My wife
has something more to tell.'

'Your wife should have told us in the first place,' said
the inspector. 'What is it now?'

'I told her who stole the blanket, Lily Conroy, and she
was wearing a green dress. She says she saw this Lily
Conroy in the green dress, picking flowers in that field
down there!'

This time the inspector bounded to his feet. Lily
Conroy was wandering about free. By now, perhaps, she
had taken off, but there was a chance that she hadn't gone
far. They must search for her without delay! There was

one other possibility and that was that she had drowned herself in the lake.

'Mrs Williams,' he said, 'you take charge of things until we come back. We're off to find this Conroy woman.'

Mary Ellen stood at the door watching them hurrying away. She wondered whether they would first search the field. Away down at the far end she was sure someone was sitting on a mound. What would a woman do if she had killed her child in a fit of temper? What, but sit in anguish and remorse, tears running down her face? Lily Conroy was by all accounts a common prostitute, but she was the mother of a baby and it seemed that she had murdered the baby.

She turned the key in the door and went out through the back garden to the field. Away down at the far end a woman in a green dress sat like a statue, staring into the distance, thinking her own terrible thoughts. Lily Conroy wasn't running away. She had come to her journey's end in a field of buttercups, half a dozen of which she had picked and held in her hand until they had wilted and toppled limply against her bony knuckles.

'I'll make you a cup of tea, dear,' said Mrs Williams, taking her by the arm. 'Come with me now. My husband will be back soon and he'll help you. There's a girl.'

Lily Conroy didn't look at the policeman's wife. She didn't give a sign that she had heard a single word, but she allowed herself to be drawn to her feet and slowly, woodenly, she walked up the field, through the back gate into the garden and at last into the police station. Once inside Mrs Williams was struck with horror at the fact that the office door was open and there, on the table, lay the dead child, but if Lily Conroy saw her baby it meant nothing to her.

'Come through here,' said the policeman's wife. 'It'll only take a minute to make the tea.'

It was an hour before P.C. Williams returned. He came

through to the kitchen and stopped in his tracks, his mouth open.

'She came to the station?' he said at length.

'No love,' said Mary Ellen. 'I went and got her from where I said she was, down in the buttercup field! She doesn't know where she is, or what she has done, poor thing. I made her a cup of tea,'

'Give her another cup!' he said. 'Don't let her out of your sight. I've got to get the inspector right away!'

The inspector came as fast as his legs would carry him. He was out of breath when he entered the room.

'You are Lily Anne Conroy?' he asked, but Lily Conroy didn't seem to hear a word.

The two policemen looked at each other.

'She'll have to be taken to Dolgellau, Williams. We'll charge her there,' said the inspector. 'Mrs Williams you've got yourself into all this. You'll have to appear in court now. I hope it isn't near your time. You've got to think of that baby of yours, too.'

'Baby?' said Lily Conroy.

She put her head in her hands and began to cry.

She was still crying when she stood in the dock, charged with taking the life of her child.

7

Troubles in Traws

OCCURRENCE BOOK ENTRY:

Henry Jones, owner of a billy goat alleged that the goat had been slaughtered without his knowledge and the dead body of the goat removed by night. I made enquiry of a number of people and a search but was unable to find the goat which I presume had strayed and was perhaps drowned in the lake.

THE goat was called Owain and P.C. Williams hadn't been long in Trawsfynydd before he came to know the animal. It was an altogether outstanding creature, high-backed, long in the leg, bright of eye. It had the look of a randy old man, someone said. It was an animal well aware of its superiority over more mundane and perhaps slightly emaciated goats such as those P.C. Williams had seen on the mountains. It had a disconcerting way of looking at people and perhaps reminding them that those fine curling horns were not entirely weapons of defence. P.C. Williams saluted the goat. He felt that having served in the Fusiliers he owed the animal that much. It deserved some respect. The goat, however, is not an animal with a particularly high intelligence and Owain had no human quality save perhaps the obstinacy of its owner. Mrs

Ellen Jones was from the very beginning the subject of complaint for half a dozen of her neighbours on either side. Owain refused to recognize natural boundaries. He ate his way through hedges and butted his way through fences. He jumped walls and walked on his hind legs to denude the trees and bushes in each garden of their foliage, and the hand of Trawsfynydd was against him, day in and day out.

'I am sorry, Policeman,' said Ellen Jones, 'but I am not going to spend money tying Owain to a post, buying a chain and keeping him from the things he likes to eat. It is for them to mend their fences and their hedges and look after their rose bushes and cabbages!'

P.C. Williams gaped and found it hard to reply immediately:

'But the goat is straying, Mrs Jones. It is making himself a great nuisance, damaging property and doing damage to bushes and vegetables and—'

'But not on the road, Policeman Williams! Not on the road and where is your business? Not in my garden. Not in the gardens of my neighbours, is it?'

'I have complaints,' he said stiffly. 'I am telling you about them. I hope that these complaints will not lead to a disturbance of the peace but if they do I will be compelled to do something about it and you have been warned.'

Mrs Jones looked grim. 'When they bring their complaints to me I will deal with them!'

P.C. Williams turned away, went into the house and took down his fishing rod.

'I have had enough, Mary Ellen,' he said. 'That Jones woman is getting my goat with her obstinate ways.'

Mary Ellen laughed at him as he took himself down the street to the bridge, watched by Owain who chewed the cud and stuck his bearded face over the top of the hedge. It was true that the trespass of the goat wasn't really his business, but he wasn't just the policeman and the representative of law in Trawsfynydd. He was the village headman and the community felt that it was his duty to resolve their difficulties.

'The Lord tempers the wind to the shorn lamb,' he said to the old man fishing from the bridge over the stream, 'but he doesn't do much about goats.'

'Don't you worry about that goat, Williams,' said the old fellow. 'The people of Traws have a way of settling things like that! A goat isn't going to make a desert of the gardens and get away with it.'

He began to fish, feeling a little more depressed as he thought about the implications of what he had heard. It meant, almost certainly, that the peace would be disturbed and perhaps 'the big man' would hear of it before he was finished.

'For heaven's sake, Williams, couldn't you have stepped in and laid the law down without all this fuss?' he would ask. 'You are supposed to prevent trouble! You are supposed to keep the peace in Traws. The militia make trouble, the Irish labourers make trouble, fair enough, but in the village, surely, you can control the few people you've got?'

Fighting Irishmen from the work schemes, soldiers from the army camp, none of these bothered him very much. He waded in and laid about him and afterwards he licked his pencil, took down their names, took statements, threatened, cautioned and, when need be, testified against the offenders when they were charged and hauled up. The goat thing was another matter. No one seemed to realize that when it boiled over and the trouble was settled they would all have to go on living with one another and maybe one or two wouldn't be able to forgive or forget.

He fished until late in the evening, taking a few trout which he carried home in his grass-lined helmet. At the top of the rise, right in the middle of Traws village there was a small crowd around the garden of Mrs Ellen Jones. Something had happened at last! He edged his way past and went into the police station, put the trout on the table, tipped the grass from his helmet and set his rod against the wall.

'They've been here for you,' said Mary Ellen. 'Shouting murder.'

'Murder?' he repeated with dismay.

Mary Ellen smiled. 'A kind of murder,' she said. 'Owain, the goat has been done in.'

He decided that he must go at once and try to meet trouble half way. The crowd around Mrs Jones's gate parted. He walked in and there was a sudden hush as he confronted the owners of the goat, Ellen Jones and her husband Harry.

'I believe you called at the station?' he asked.

'I called!' said Harry Jones, his small eyes glittering. 'I called, and you weren't there!'

'I am here now,' he said, stating the obvious. 'Tell me what it's all about.'

'Our goat has been killed!'

He pointed to the dead animal. Owain's life blood had pumped away through a gash in his hairy throat. He was quite dead, and in death he looked sad, pathetic, a caricature of his former self, kneeling as he was on his forelegs, with his head lying on the grass.

'Murdered!' shouted Harry Jones.

'By one of this lot!' shouted his wife, waving her arm at the onlookers.

'He deserved it!' shouted one of the hostile crowd. 'He bloody well did!'

'That will do,' said P.C. Williams, taking out his notebook and fumbling for his pencil. 'Now, at what time did this happen?'

'Ask him!' shouted Ellen Jones, pointing to a man in the crowd.

'I better talk to you one at a time in the office,' he said, looking steadily at the man at whom the accusing finger was pointing.

'Take them all in!' shouted Harry Jones. 'I want them all charged with killing this animal.'

'Hold on, hold on,' said P.C. Williams. 'You charge one, you make a complaint. I'll listen.'

'I make a complaint as well!' shrieked Ellen Jones.

'I'll take note of the complaint and hear your allegation in the office, but I want to know who is the owner of the goat for a start!'

'We are both the owners of the goat,' shouted Harry Jones.

'Then who will I record in my book as the person making the allegations?'

'I am making the complaint!' shrieked Ellen Jones. 'Murderers!'

'I am making the complaint!' corrected Harry Jones. 'I, I am the alligator!'

The crowd milled around Ellen Jones and her husband as they followed in procession to the police station.

'Very well, Harry Jones,' said the constable passing a hand over his mouth. 'You are the alligator, but now, since you are, you must give me reasons for accepting this complaint. I don't deny that the goat is dead or that its throat was cut. I don't suggest that you or your wife did it, but you must have some person or persons against whom you make the complaint, unless you are asking me to investigate and discover whether there is evidence to support a prosecution.'

'Put me down as the alligator,' said Harry Jones. 'That's the first thing, and I accuse everybody in Traws!'

'We'll have to narrow it down a bit,' said P.C. Williams, recording the fact in the Occurrence Book. 'I'll make some inquiries.'

The crowd at the door fell back before the fury of

Ellen Jones and her husband as the two took themselves off to their own door. P.C. Williams went out into the road and looked at the sky. Bats were flying. It would soon be quite dark.

'Tomorrow morning,' he said. 'I can't do anything tonight.'

When they had gone to bed he and Mary Ellen became hysterical with laughter at the remarks of Jones the Alligator. In the morning the case became a little more complicated for, to the delight of the neighbours, the corpse of Owain the billygoat had vanished in the night. There wasn't a bit of evidence to be found, not so much as a hair of the goat, and the soil upon which he had poured out his blood had been dug up and removed into the bargain.

'Have you seen anything of the goat that was lying in Jones's garden last night?' he asked them all, one after another.

'Never noticed the goat,' they said. 'I expect it wandered away somewhere!'

'Come on, now,' he said angrily. 'You know what it is to obstruct a policeman in the execution of his duty?'

'We saw the goat,' they said. 'Maybe it was just sick. Maybe it got up and walked away.'

The goat, with a heavy rock tied to its body, was no doubt deep in the water of the lake, or in some bog hole not far away. Things had changed, however. What about the entry in the book now? He thought about it and went back to Ellen Jones.

'You can't get far with this thing,' he said. 'The goat was killed but you need its body for proof. All we've got is a missing goat.'

'We haven't got a goat at all!' shouted Jones the Alligator. 'You should have taken charge of it. It was evidence.'

'It was on your property and there was no suggestion that you wanted it removed,' he said.

'I'll write to the Chief Constable,' Ellen Jones promised.

'You do that, Mrs Jones,' he said. 'I'm sure he'll take notice of the complaint. He always does.'

The way that he said it left Ellen Jones and her husband in some doubt as to the wisdom of taking the matter farther. Already Harry Jones had earned himself a name in the community, one that he would carry to the grave, Jones the Alligator, and Ellen his wife, Mrs Jones the Alligator. In Wales nicknames show no pity. They are given with little compassion. A man earns one and he may as easily lose his fingerprints or a birthmark!

Jones the Alligator wasn't the only native of the place to earn a name for himself during the service of P.C. Williams. Evan Roberts was to achieve a similar distinction. Evan was the epitome of a henpecked husband. Day in and day out his wife scolded him. Night after night their differences rose to a crescendo and a climax during which Mrs Evan Roberts was never able to resist giving her spouse the hammering of his life. She blacked one eye and then the other. She tugged hair from his head. She ripped the vest from his back. She drummed his head against the wall of the bedroom, or rattled his skull on the floor. When Evan escaped her clutches he ran protesting to P.C. Williams.

'Come back with me and stop her hitting me again!' he said. 'She'll kill me!' and P.C. Williams, pulling his trousers and tunic on, would march down the street and enter the dark, silent cottage of Mr and Mrs Evan Roberts.

'Now Mrs Roberts,' he would say, 'I have another complaint against you. You must not use violence on your husband like this. The next time I will accept the complaint. I'll put it down and you'll be charged with assault, grievous bodily harm, breach of the peace. . .'

He could think of no more and invariably at this stage Mrs Evan Roberts saw the error of her ways, pulled her nightgown about her and went meekly upstairs, her husband following her a little nervously.

The trouble was never known to break out more than once a night, but the duty irked P.C. Williams as much as any trouble that the Irish labourers and the rough soldiery brought upon him on Saturday nights. Sometimes, aware of the first murmuring of the conflict away down at the far end of the street, P.C. Williams was unable to get his sleep because he waited restlessly for the summons. Mary Ellen was disturbed by it in a similar way and her hands were so fully occupied by day—she had by this time borne three more daughters, Dulcie Muriel in 1920, Sylvia May in 1922 and Vera Margaret in 1923—that she could ill-afford to lose her precious sleep.

Evan Roberts was less than a man, P.C. Williams would remark when he heard the knocking at his door at midnight or one o'clock in the morning and had to lever himself out of bed to answer the summons.

Evan Roberts took the chastisement of the policeman as meekly as he took the assaults of his wife.

'Be a man, Evan! Stand up for yourself. Give her a black eye before she gives you two. Don't come here knocking on my door every night. You're a disgrace. That's what you are! I feel like giving you a wallop on my own account! Do you think I got nothing better to do than persuade your wife to leave off knocking you about and let you get into bed with her! What about my wife? She feels the cold when I come back to bed. She gets awakened too! I've got eight children in this house. They get disturbed, all because you're a gutless creature not fit to be called a man and come running to me!'

'I got a right to police protection,' Evan Roberts said.

There was nothing that the policeman could say to that,

but he found that each time Evan Roberts came to complain his own reaction became more and more hostile.

'I'll give him a good hiding!' he told Mary Ellen.

The village policeman of his father's generation would not have hesitated to act as judge, jury and executioner, but P.C. Williams was reluctant to take the law into his own hands. He was equally reluctant to press the inspector to proceed with charges which, when Evan Roberts and his wife had cooled down, would surely fall apart for lack of substantiation. Disturbing the peace in Traws was a charge that no one higher up expected him to bring forward except against incomers.

At last a night in the saga of Evan Roberts's marital wars arrived to strain the policeman's patience beyond its limits. It was half-past one. The village slept in the soft light of the moon. Away out on the moorland sheep bleated and owls hunted along the drystone walls, calling to one another occasionally. In the backyard henruns a few rats scuttled. There was nothing to alarm them until Mrs Evan Roberts drove her husband out of her bed, her bedroom and her house, and there he stood in his grey flannel shirt, nursing a cut above his left eye. He had nowhere to go but to the police station. He went gingerly up the road in his bare feet. The breeze blew his shirt tails and goosepimples stood on his legs. He shivered. His knocking on the door set the Williams' dog barking, a hollow sound that soon brought the policeman to his wits. He rubbed sleep from his eyes and lay for a moment wondering what the caller might want and then, as he discounted one thing and then another, he told himself with a burning anger that this was Evan Roberts again, and this time he would get what he deserved!

Evan Roberts waited, shivering more and more. P.C. Williams pulled on his trousers, slipped his braces over his shoulders, cursed the man who knocked and made the dog bark. The children were beginning to awaken. It was more than flesh and blood could be expected to stand! It was an outrage! The fact that the caller could have been any other than Evan Roberts had gone from his mind like one of the silvery clouds scudding across the bowl of the moonlit sky. This was Evan Roberts and, fair play to him, he was going to get the reception he really asked for!

For a Welshman his own language is the only one in which he can really express deep emotion. Words of love sound insincere to him unless they are spoken in his native tongue. It is much the same when it comes to the expression of anger. P.C. Williams opened the door, saw Evan Roberts and unleashed upon him such an attack as the poor man had never suffered from his wife. The eloquence of the policeman's address might have held the judges at an Eisteddfod. It was in its own right a veritable poem of rage to which there was no reply. Evan Roberts bowed under it and when it was at an end he muttered, 'I am entitled to—' but he got no further than that. P.C. Williams grabbed him, whirled him about to throw him from the door, drawing back to plant a hard kick on his backside. It was at that point that Evan earned the nickname he carried to the grave, Evan Ironarse, for the policeman's bare foot missed its target and came full force against the jamb of the door. Evan Ironarse ran for his life. P.C. Williams collapsed on the ground, his eyes suddenly filled with tears of pain, the bones of his big toe dislocated. The dog in the kitchen cocked its ear and began to whine with anxiety. Upstairs Mary Ellen turned over, listened for a moment or two, and concluded that Arthur had lost his temper and knocked poor Evan Roberts down. There was a draught blowing up through the house. She wished that her husband would settle the matter and come back to bed. She badly wanted to sleep.

P.C. Williams sat nursing his burst toe for a while and then he struggled to stand and then to hop to the stair, forgetting that the door was still open. He dragged himself upstairs and at last sat on the bed, moaning pitifully at the pain in his foot.

'I'll murder Evan Roberts!' he said. 'I'll swing for him!'

'What has he done to you?' asked Mary Ellen.

The thought that a man like Evan Roberts could have done anything to him made P.C. Williams laugh despite his pain.

'I went to kick his backside,' he said ruefully. 'It wasn't where I thought it was! I kicked the door. I think I've broken my toe.'

Mary Ellen got out of bed and lit a candle so that she could examine her husband's injured foot.

'Dear me,' she said, 'I think maybe you have. You'll never get your boot on!'

'All I want is to get back to bed and for the pain to stop.'

Mary Ellen said he would have to get the doctor in the morning. Their doctor lived in Ffestiniog. He never sent a bill. It was his rule never to charge a policeman's family for treatment. He observed the same rule for the impoverished clergy.

The implications of his injury slowly dawned on P.C. Williams. He wouldn't be able to make his rounds either on his bicycle or on foot. He wouldn't be able to meet the sergeant. There would have to be some explanation for his inability to perform his daily task. Something would have to go down in the book. He considered the business of Evan Roberts. The Occurrence Book entry would read, 'It was reported to me that Evan Roberts's wife had shut the complainant out in his nightclothes. He came to ask me to persuade her to let him re-enter his house. As I hurried to go with him, forgetting that I had no boots on, my foot came in contact with the doorsill. My great toe was severely damaged. I was unable to investigate the incident further, but I was told later that

Mrs Evan Roberts admitted her husband to the house and the complaint was withdrawn.'

In the morning the doctor looked at his foot.

'Williams,' he said, 'I would say you took a flying kick at somebody. You didn't just stub your toe, did you?'

'Look, doctor,' he said, looking sheepish, 'I stubbed my toe.'

'You stubbed your toe very badly! I'll leave a note you can show to your superiors, but anybody can tell you were in a hurry when you did it, the way you might be trying to convert a try!'

The village might have been asleep but somehow the story got out. The policeman had broken his toe on Evan's backside. He might have been soft in the face of his wife's attack, but in retreat Evan was a man of iron—Evan Ironarse! There were some who couldn't help laughing, but P.C. Williams wasn't quite so ready to laugh in public. Sooner or later the sergeant and the inspector would come across the nickname and the story would go round the whole Constabulary—Williams broke his big toe on the backside of a man who wanted him to accept a complaint! The Chief might get to hear about it.

'Williams,' said the Chief when, in his mind, he stood on the carpet in the office of the Chief Constable, Dolgellau, 'Williams, you know how a complaint should be received. You know what you are supposed to do when a member of the public comes to you and asks for your assistance in a domestic matter? You know that you are not supposed to use violence against him? You know that you are leaving the police open to charges? You know that you can be dismissed from the Force for a thing like this and that damages can be awarded against you and against this Force?'

He slumped in despair at the thought. Sacked, a man with eight children! He had never known what it was to be in disgrace. He had kept his nose clean until now. Somehow, however, every small cloud on the horizon indicated disaster. He invariably saw dismissal ahead. Men had gone out of the Force for much less!

'No, sir,' he said to the grim figure of the Chief. 'I did not kick him. I ordered him out. I had had hundreds of complaints which I knew wouldn't stand up in court. I certainly bundled him out of the door. I kicked the woodwork of the door . . . I wasn't really trying to kick him. Would I, sir, with no boot on my foot?'

And the imaginary scene faded. The Chief Constable had signalled that he was to go. His job was still his!

The inspector came in due course. He looked at the swollen foot, stretching the woollen sock far beyond anything that might have been squeezed into a boot.

'Tell me, Williams,' he said, 'did you kick his backside or not?'

'I missed it, sir,' he said, 'or this wouldn't have happened.'

'True,' said the inspector. 'True, but then look what might have happened. Mrs Evan Roberts might have had you up in court for damaging her poor husband.'

P.C. Williams sighed. He was thankful that everyone looked at it in the most favourable light. Evan Ironarse seemed to walk a little taller thereafter. Mrs Evan Roberts scowled when she heard the nickname but no one considered her feelings. She came to regard her diminutive husband with more respect. Evan looked at P.C. Williams when, as he recuperated, he hobbled down the village street on his stick, and in a strange way was thankful to him.

They stopped and had a few words with each other.

'Now, Ironarse,' said the policeman, 'I don't expect you'll ever give me a second chance.'

'I won't,' said Evan. 'We learnt our lesson, teh?'

The impudence of the little man made P.C. Williams

laugh. He held no malice. After all, the injury he had suffered had saved him from something much worse. Keeping the peace was what mattered. Only occasionally did he have to use force and almost invariably it was against an outsider and a stranger in the place.

Strangers in the place were not uncommon, however, for the expansion of the army camp near by, and the labour force engaged on building the camp swelling accordingly, resulted in an influx of both soldiers and navvies. They vied with one another in drinking ale and fighting. They lingered on in the village when most people had gone to sleep, smoking, talking, drinking from bottles, arguing, fighting, falling down and sleeping by a hedge or wall and awakening in the small hours to sing, or complain, as the mood took them. P.C. Williams's job was a twenty-four hours a day stint. Sleeping and eating were incidental so far as authority was concerned. He was there to be on call whenever needed. His task was to see that sleeping dogs were let lie and unruly dogs were put on the chain!

There is a certain type of man to whom a policeman's uniform is something like a red flag to a bull. He sees the man in the uniform and not what he stands for. He wants to reduce the policeman to his own level and no opportunity to challenge him can be allowed to pass. In fact, where there is no challenge, one must be offered. P.C. Williams found that the words above the door of the house were enough—County Police Station, Merioneth Constabulary. Again and again trouble came to his door. Soldiers who had had too much to drink lounged against the wall and cursed authority until he came to deal with them. Navvies who had been seeing red for hours sought release in a hand-to-hand struggle in the road where the policeman could not turn a blind eye. P.C. Williams obliged. He gave them their little wrestling matches, took them in, chastised them, threatened them, turned them loose and pacified them with soft words when he felt that this was more prudent than provoking a riot. Not every soldier complained with comrades at his elbow to see him fight the policeman. Now and again a solitary soldier, a morose outcast, came to demonstrate that he was a lone wolf. Such a one knocked on the door at two o'clock in the morning when everyone else, the last of the befuddled navvies, had taken themselves off. For this solitary fellow a challenge at the police station was preferable to a challenge at the main gate of the camp, or an attempt to straddle the barbed-wire apron surrounding the place.

'Open up!' he shouted. 'I want a bed for the night. Open up in the King's name!'

P.C. Williams opened his bedroom window and looked down. He could see the brass on the soldier's hat, the sturdy figure in tunic and puttees.

'Go away!' he said.

The soldier began to hammer on the door again. 'A bed for the night!' he yelled, adding a few words that were intended to convey doubt about the validity of the policeman's birth certificate.

P.C. Williams didn't wait to put on his trousers but raced downstairs in his shirt tails and threw open the door. The battle began there and then. The army retreated, through the gate, down the road, yard after yard of rearguard action in the face of superior enemy pressure. The wind blew on the tall policeman's hairy legs and the stones hurt his feet, but he was never one to consider minor discomfort when the battle was going his way. At last the hardy soldier, battered and bleeding, decided that he would surrender. P.C. Williams led him meekly by the hand back to the office where he handcuffed him to a heavy chair.

'Now see,' he said, 'I'll take you back to camp in the morning and put nothing in the book. I've been in the army myself, even if I never got stupid drunk like you, so you sleep it off here. Use that bucket if you need to, and let me get my rest until the morning, teh?'

The soldier nodded and slumped back in the chair. In the morning P.C. Williams, with a fine black eye of his own and a prisoner much the worse for wear, marched to Trawsfynydd Camp and handed his prisoner over to the military.

'Deserter,' said the sergeant-major. 'Come to take his punishment at last.'

'Sign for him then, if you please,' said the policeman.

'You got any charges against him?'

The policeman smiled. 'No,' he said. 'So far as I am concerned he's been punished.'

'So have you,' said the sergeant-major.

His inspector looked at the black eye. 'Williams,' he said, 'maybe you need a holiday, eh? We got something in mind for you. . .'

In due course he discovered what that something was.

8

Bread Without Weight

OCCURRENCE BOOK ENTRY:

Accused denied the offence and said, Your something scales are wrong then and you got no right to charge me. Anybody will tell you that some loaves is lighter than others.

'A LITTLE walking tour, Williams,' said the Superintendent. 'You like walking, eh? Your feet don't bother you?'

'Only my breath, sir,' he said. 'Since I came back it hasn't got any better.'

'Well save your breath to cool your porridge, Williams, eh?'

A Superintendent could make any sort of joke he liked even if he hadn't been almost shaken out of his wits in shellholes, and never able to catch his breath properly since.

'Yes, sir,' he said, standing as straight as a telegraph pole, as a constable did in the presence of higher ranks.

'You won't have to hurry, Williams, and the weather is warm and sunny. You go from place to place, reporting to the office when you have booked offenders and supplying the necessary statements for proceedings, at which you will be the chief witness. You can dress for the part. You have some old clothes?'

Some old clothes? He could hardly help smiling. It was hard to keep one very old suit of civilian clothes respectable enough for a walk down the village. He went to church on Sunday in his uniform. A man with eight children didn't worry about not having old clothes! He worried about only having old clothes, if he worried about that sort of thing at all. Mary Ellen, proud and neat, expert with her needle though she was, had to dress in old clothes to keep the children respectable. A policeman's children had to look respectable. They were part of his image. They were the background of his respectability.

'Dressed like a tramp, you should pass,' said the Superintendent, 'and with your warrant card you can cope with anything that may arise. The scales and weights will be in your sack, which you will carry over your back. I think it's an excellent scheme. You'll set off on Monday. We'll take in Traws from Tanygrisau. It won't do the man there any harm to stretch his legs and see a bit more.'

P.C. Williams nodded. He hardly dared express concern for his beat. There were things and people around Trawsfynydd that needed careful and diplomatic handling. A policeman from outside could do a lot of harm. But there was no help for it. *They* decided these things. He was in no position to question the wisdom of what they did.

'About lodgings, sir?' he asked at last.

'Ah yes,' said the Superintendent. 'That is a little problem. We'll have to sort that out. We can't have you being taken into the cells as a vagrant every night! You must look and behave like a tramp in every way. We'll think about that.'

He hoped they would think about it without too much

delay. He didn't fancy sleeping out. Mary Ellen would have something to say about that! He didn't see himself in a flea-ridden workhouse bed. Fleas had been all very well in France. Everyone had had them there. It was said that even a Staff Officer had been seen to scratch himself, miles behind the line, but even though he was looking forward to what they called a walking tour of North Wales he was determined to do it in comfort as far as he could, and come back home without workhouse fleas.

'You'd better take a spare pair of boots,' said Mary Ellen, 'and a change of clothes, a towel and some soap—'

'A carpet bag for my stuff and the sack with the old iron scales on my other shoulder, eh? I'd look like something then! Everybody would stare at me. It wouldn't be long before I was attracting attention. First place I went to they'd weigh me up—'

He laughed at his own joke. Weigh him up. What he was supposed to do was to buy a loaf of bread, see whether the baker or the grocer put it on his scales, warn him that he would be charged for not weighing it if he neglected to do so. If the bread happened to be weighed in his presence he must take it outside, weigh it on his own scales and check that the weights used by the baker were accurate. There were two charges, selling bread without the use of weights, and selling bread short of the statutory weights of large and small loaves. It seemed that nowhere in North Wales was the letter of the law being observed, but, much worse, in many places the public were being sold short weight.

'The first thing that will happen to you, love,' said Mary Ellen, 'is that somebody will hit you over the head thinking you've come to steal, or some policeman will run you in and leave you in the cell all night.'

He had thought about that and smiled to himself. He had his warrant card, but a new thought struck him. If he fell into the hands of some village constable the village would see him arrested and wonder about his release perhaps. The village baker would be on his guard and perhaps refuse to sell him a loaf, making him tramp on miles and miles to the next place and, worst of all, he would have to report failure in this particular instance. A tramp he would be. The warrant card would be his last resort!

'Monday morning I'm on my way,' he said. 'By Monday they'll have sorted out how the expenses are to be paid. I'll need money for bed, and money for food. I'll need money for bread. But they can't expect me to eat all the loaves I buy in places with two or three bread shops, can they?'

Mary Ellen thought this very funny. She said she wouldn't put it past them. They would perhaps give him money for cheese or butter! He didn't laugh when she suggested he send the bread home in parcels. Short-weight bread wasn't reliable as evidence in court, the Superintendent had warned him. Bread dried out. The weighing and checking, once he had found evidence of short weight, had to be done again in the presence of the vendor. Any dispute then would be over the discrepancy in the scales. Since the scales he carried would be accurate, the case for the magistrates would be straightforward, although the baker's continued use of his faulty scales might create a problem.

The money for his night's lodging plus his dinner arrived at the police station in time for his departure. His itinerary had been worked out and arrangements made for him to draw money at other places along the way. The Superintendent had no intention of risking his tramp detective being robbed by some genuine vagrant, for then the whole thing would become a joke against the Force and the Chief Constable would take a serious view of anything of that sort.

'Good luck then, Williams,' said the inspector when he

had handed over the instructions. 'Don't get run in, and send us a postcard, teh?'

He promised to do that. At his first stopping place he went to the post office, where they sold bread.

'A penny stamp,' he said, 'this postcard and a loaf, please.'

The bread was put on the scales. He paid for it and stood writing his postcard to his old friend, Bob Walmsley in Blaenau. Having a lovely time, wish you were here. Bob would be puzzled at first, wondering how he managed to get off when he was stuck on the beat.

Walking a short distance along the road he opened his sack, took out his scales and weighed the bread. It was a little over the weight and he was disappointed. He put away the scales, dropping the loaf into the sack, and sat down to make his first written report: 'Rhyd y Maen. Bread purchased was weighed and subsequently I checked the weight. It was one ounce above the pound.' As he wrote he thought how the story of his walking tour would pass through the Merioneth Constabulary. Old Dick Hughes who had followed him at Penrhyndeudraeth would laugh his head off, and Glyn Humphries from Bala would make jokes about him for the rest of his days unless he could book at least a score of offenders. Supposing someone had passed the word around, and all the bakers in North Wales were making sure that, just for once, for the brief period in which the Constabulary were checking up, everyone was getting full measure? The boys would laugh and say, 'Put P.C. Williams on the road again. He likes eating loaves. He's got eight children. Got to keep his strength up. . .'

Grimly he slung the sack over his shoulder and strode on. There was no smoke without fire, even from a village bakery chimney. Before noon he stopped and looked into his sack. They had said nothing about the bread and he could do what he liked with it. He had no butter, but the bread was new and the smell of it made his mouth water. He began to pull it apart and eat it. They wouldn't mind him staying his hunger, would they? A loaf cost only a few pennies and the road was long! A sparrow came from nowhere to beg a crumb, and then, startling him because he had walked the grass verge to approach, a tramp.

'Spare a bit for me, chum?' he asked.

Chum. An old soldier by the cut of him. He tore a piece from the loaf and offered it. His companion took it and ate greedily.

'Where you get it?' he asked.

'Post office back there,' he said.

They ate for a while in silence.

'What you got in the sack?'

The sack quite obviously didn't contain clothes, but some solid, angular object and the tramp's sharp eyes were upon it.

'Something I'm going to sell,' he said. 'When I get a chance.'

'Let's see it then!'

He stood up. 'No,' he said. 'It's my business.'

'Copper down there is a mate of mine,' said the other. 'Knows me well. I might tip him off, see?'

'You tip him off,' he promised, 'and I'll come after you!'

He swung the sack and by accident the scales struck the other man in the chest.

'Here!' he said, springing up.

The policeman looked him in the eye and somehow the angry tramp recognized a certain authority that disturbed him.

'I'll fix you, mate,' he said, backing off.

P.C. Williams walked on alone, leaving the tramp leaning against the drystone wall, watching him. The hungry sparrow still fed on crumbs lying in the grit at the roadside.

At his next port of call the bread wasn't weighed and

when he checked the weight of the loaf he had paid for he found that it was two ounces below the pound.

'I have to inform you,' he said, 'that I am a police officer. You have supplied bread without weighing it in my presence. The weight of the bread has been checked by me. It is below the statutory limit, and I will show you on these scales, which have been checked and are stamped, that the bread you have sold is underweight. I must warn you that you will be charged with both offences and anything you say will be taken down by me and may be used in evidence.'

The baker stared at him open-mouthed. 'I thought you were a poor tramp,' he said. 'I thought you were hungry and didn't take time to weigh the bread—'

'I see,' he said. 'You knew I was coming and saved a short-weight loaf for me?'

'All right,' said the baker. 'What can I say? The only thing I might say would make you book me again, but you know what I think of you!'

'I know what you think of me,' he said. 'I know what I think of you. I look at the sort of people you're taking money from, and how badly they need bread. What I think of you I won't get a chance to say, even in court. That's what grieves me!'

A hundred yards further down the street he bought another loaf. It was like catching fish in the river on a perfect fishing day. Once again the bread was delivered over the counter without going on the scales and proved to be underweight. He went through the formula and cautioned the grocer.

'You picked on me!' said the angry man. 'What about him up the street?'

'I picked on him too! You'll have company when you come up, I expect. Two places selling bread and both of them short-weight. I'm glad I don't live here.'

'You couldn't live anywhere! You'd be run out!'

He was used to abuse. It ran off him like water off a duck's back, and he knew that if he liked he could provoke most people into giving grounds for a further charge. It wasn't his way, however. Live and let live—within the law—was a sound enough maxim. He had his job to do and most decent people realized that. Now that he could record two successful cases he wasn't worried about the initial failure. After all, there were more honest men in the world than there were thieves. A man had to believe that or there was no point in going to church on Sunday. There was no hope for mankind otherwise.

As he strode on he became aware that he was being dogged by someone who contrived to keep just as far behind as he could, but still keep contact. He guessed who it was, the tramp with whom he had shared the first loaf. Now he had two loaves, two cases. It would be highly inconvenient to make a third out of this fellow who seemed determined either to find out what he had in his sack, or steal the sack. Once again he thought of an imaginary report: 'I had the scales in the sack and was resting when I suddenly discovered that the sack was missing. I had earlier noticed that I was being followed. I reported my loss to the constable at. . .' He shuddered at the thought. What would the Superintendent say?

'Williams, you allowed this tramp to steal up on you and take the scales! You book two cases, and the scales, a vital part of the evidence against these two offenders, are stolen from you! I thought you were a man with his wits about him! When the Chief hears about this you'll be on the carpet, out of the Force!'

This kind of thought had always troubled him. The sack, dismissal from the Force, was his eternal nightmare and he could never counteract it with the certain knowledge that he was a man who did his duty and had always done it. There was only one way to settle this business. He must take a rest, pretend to sleep on some gorse-grown knoll and allow his persecutor to sneak up and steal the sack! If he could bring things to a head all would be well, and there would be no need to come out of his disguise as a tramp, for he would hammer the thief until he couldn't stand on his feet.

It was a pleasant little place he chose, climbing over the wall and going uphill through the short green bracken and the ferns. Birds sang in the thorn hedge and the air was full of the heavy scent of may blossom. He put the sack down, stretched himself at full length and lay back looking at the blue sky and the cotton wool clouds through half-closed eyes. His feet were tired. He was ready to sleep. There was no need to pretend, and then, all at once, he was asleep!

When he awoke he grabbed for the sack, but it wasn't there. It was gone! He looked up at the sky that seemed suddenly black. The tramp had managed it, but how long ago? How many minutes had passed? The birds seemed to be singing just as merrily. Often birdsong changed as the day grew older. The sun seemed to be in the same place in the heavens, and then he detected movement away along the side of the field, among the bracken. The thief was there, crouched down, examining the contents of the sack. The thing to do was to get to him as quietly as possible. He undid his bootlaces, slipped his boots off, got to his feet and began to run with long, loping strides, going silently across the grass. The tramp who had tipped out the scales was eating bread when the shadow of the policeman fell upon him. He gaped and choked and finally spoke.

'You won't get much for a set of bloody scales and weights,' he said. 'I thought you'd got something good, and bread! You're good at pinching bread!'

He didn't wait to hear more but dragged the fellow to his feet. 'Right,' he said. 'You'll take your punishment here and now!'

The battle, for the tramp was no coward, swayed one way and then the other. His sudden rush across the field had inhibited the policeman's breathing, it wasn't just that he was ageing, growing old in the service, as he jokingly put it, but he was no longer the fit young fellow who had marched off with the Fusiliers. He didn't have a disability pension for nothing and such strenuous exertion didn't make combat easy, but at last the tramp began to fall down more quickly than he got up. A bruise over one eye was matched by a swelling under the other. His nose bled and at last he didn't get up any more. P.C. Williams licked his broken knuckles.

'I don't want to sort you out again,' he said, 'but if you want more, just you keep on my trail, only make sure I'm sounder asleep next time because if I'm not you'll have more than a black eye. You won't be able to walk after me!'

His anger didn't leave him until he was well along the road. The nightmare thoughts he had had returned again and again when he considered the disaster which could so easily have befallen him in his scheme to rid himself of the persistent tramp.

That night he wrote a card to his wife and assured her that he was well, feeling the benefit of a walk in the country. He addressed it simply to Mrs M. Williams Trawsfynydd. The earlier cards he had sent to friends in the Force had given no hint that the sender was a policeman, or that the recipients were constables in the Force, for he didn't need to be told that in villages the postman could hardly help but read a postcard and impart its message to interested parties on his round . . . 'Policeman Williams is away from home, see? Playing the detective I've heard. Doesn't look like a detective to me, though. Don't reckon he'll catch nobody. A detective looks like a detective, I mean to say. . .'

The following day he booked three more bakers. It

was time to send more substantial evidence to Dolgellau.
He reported at a police station and showed his warrant
card. The constable stared at him.

'Well, well,' he said. 'Nobody told me. You reckon
you need all that bread? I could do with a couple of them
old loaves to feed my hens, teh? Put you up for the night
if you like, Twenty-one.'

He put away the warrant, which had been duly inspected.

'Make some toast for the children,' he said. 'Too good
for the hens.'

He tipped five loaves on to the table and the constable
felt them.

'They make lovely bread around here,' he said. 'Makes
your mouth water. Best bread in Merioneth they make.'

'Only they don't weigh it, or check their scales! Careless lot, teh? I got a fair bag. Got to get the papers off to
Dolgellau. You let me have your table for an hour?'

He sat down and began outlining his inquiries and the
results obtained. There was ample evidence for the first
five of no less than a hundred prosecutions that would
mark his tour through North Wales. The Chief Constable
would look at the figures, happy in the thought that,
whatever they were doing over in Caernarvonshire, when
H.M. Inspector of Constabulary came round he couldn't
fail to notice that Merioneth had been doing its bit, and
there, you could buy a loaf without being done.

'We got bread and jam, bread and butter, bread and
cheese, toast and just plain bread,' said the constable in
charge when he joined him for a meal.

The constable's wife blushed. It was almost true. She,
like his own wife, was hard pressed to find enough to
feed her family. Visitors were welcome to what there was,
but there wasn't much. There never could be on sixty
shillings a week with food, clothes and other things to
be paid for.

'Bread pudding tomorrow,' said the constable. 'Pity you can't send some back on the bus.'

'All the spare bread goes back to the Chief at Dolgellau,' he laughed. 'He's got children too, and hens, and poor relations.'

They all laughed. The following day he was on his way, further along the quiet roads of the county, carrying his sack, plodding on. Soon he was to be involved in a situation that had dogged him from the first stage of his journey.

'Well,' said the young constable, stepping out of the gateway and grabbing him by the arm, 'I've been waiting for you!'

The law had caught up with itself at last!

P.C. Williams looked beyond the constable to the tramp he had met on the road outside Rhyd y Maen and held his tongue.

'What you got in this sack?'

He opened the sack and revealed the contents.

'A pair of scales and five loaves of bread! Right then, you'll come along with me!'

He was thinking to himself that Christ might have been arrested for having loaves and fishes, had he encountered such a short-sighted, over-zealous young constable as this one. The tramp he had given a black eye smiled sourly at him, thinking that at last he had got his own back. There was more to it, of course.

'This man said you assaulted him in a field near Rhyd y Maen on 3 June.'

'If you're going to make charges,' he said, laughing inwardly, 'then maybe you should caution me, eh?'

The young constable pulled him by the arm, took charge of the sack and ordered him to be on his way along to the station. It was obvious that he was swelling with importance. He had caught a tramp, a felon, it seemed, a man who stole a set of scales and then went along helping himself to bread from village shops. There was this complaint, too, if someone could substantiate what the other fellow said. It had looked like a dull day, but now, thanks to Providence and a willing informant, he had made an arrest! There might even be a commendation in it. Mentally, as though he had read the young constable's mind, P.C. Williams was running through this train of thought. He wouldn't show the constable his warrant. He was under no compulsion to do so. To preserve his identity as a tramp it was even in the interests of the Superintendent and higher-ups that he kept silent, at least until someone of a higher rank asked questions.

'Get in there, then!' ordered the young constable when he reached the police station.

'I'm arrested then?'

'You're being held while I make further inquiries.'

'On what charge? I haven't been cautioned. I haven't been charged. You tell me what I'm supposed to have done!'

'Being in possession of these scales, obviously the property of some Government department, is enough for me! You'll wait there until I find out more about you. First off, your name?'

'Arthur Howell Williams,' he said; and then, smiling to himself again, he added, 'No fixed abode.'

The young constable hadn't asked him to empty his pockets. It was plain that he had jumped to the conclusion that a vagrancy charge could be added to all the other bits he had in mind. The door closed and P.C. Arthur Howell Williams settled down to watch a fly climbing the window. He was enjoying himself much more than he had done since leaving home. Here was a story they could send round Merioneth when the time came—Williams the Bread, under lock and key, charged with having a set of scales in his possession, bread stolen from a shop, having no visible means of support! It wouldn't get that far, of course, for no sergeant would accept charges without seeing what he had in his pockets and asking for a statement regarding his movements. Then there was the outlook of the higher-ups. They might see the joke, but they wouldn't expect it to go further than an explanation to the constable's sergeant. That moment wouldn't be long in coming. In the meantime Williams took his ease, listening to the children playing in the street outside, and somewhere close at hand, a bantam cock crowing every now and again.

'Right then,' said the inspector who opened the door. 'Stand up when I speak to you! You say your name is Arthur Howell Williams, no fixed abode? You have in your possession this sack and a set of scales, five loaves of bread. How do you explain them?'

'P.C. Arthur Howell Williams, sir,' he said, bringing his warrant card out of his pocket and watching the face of the young constable.

The inspector's mouth fell open. He looked at the warrant.

'Come on, come on,' he said. 'Where did you obtain this card? You know it's an offence to represent yourself to be a police officer?'

'Yes sir. I remember reading the charge, Unlawfully and falsely representing yourself to be Police Officer of the Merioneth Constabulary, Section 15, County Police Act 1839—'

The inspector suddenly looked angry. 'You are a policeman! Why did you allow yourself to be arrested? What are you supposed to be doing, dressed as a tramp and carrying scales in a sack?'

'Checking the sale of bread by weight, sir.'

'*Anwyl!* I forgot! I had a note about it! All right Williams, get out! Don't give my constables so much trouble in future.'

P.C. Williams picked up his sack and winked at the young constable.

'You got a complaint against me?' he asked.

The young constable looked sheepish. He was remembering all the little things about his 'tramp' that might have revealed him for what he was, that stuff about cautioning, about the charges.

'You hurry on down the road after your informant,' said P.C. Williams. 'Bring him back and go through his pockets. I'll take a bet you'll find a big bunch of keys he couldn't explain, and maybe a picklock in the other pocket. One thing you can be sure of, he hasn't got a warrant he can flash to get out of trouble.'

The crestfallen constable suddenly smiled. 'I wish I could slap a charge on you,' he said, 'but if I can't have you I'll have your mate!'

'You do that,' said Williams. 'Get the beggar off my heels before I have to belt him again, and keep him inside, or he'll try getting me arrested everywhere I go.'

Shortly afterwards, on his way to his next port of call, P.C. Williams met the young constable hauling his prisoner back to the police station. He couldn't resist a last little joke:

'Don't worry,' he called to the tramp. 'You got half-a-crown he'll let you go. Offer him half-a-crown, see? I got off.'

He could almost see the bribe being offered. The young constable said nothing.

There were other occasions when he had to explain himself, but he wasn't taken in again. The word had got round and even if the bakers and bakery-owners didn't know him, constables in the little towns of Merioneth spotted the bread detective as he came into their parish, and went out of their way to avoid him so that he could make his purchase and move on. Old, regular tramps who were chivvied along the road might have been puzzled to see how policemen, who persecuted them and hounded them along from one place to another, passed the tramp with the sack on the other side of the road.

When the score was over a hundred and he had done all he could to remedy the defect in the commercial enterprise of selling bread, P.C. Williams turned himself in the direction of home. He sat on the one-man bus that rocked and swayed through the quiet countryside between his point of embarkation and Trawsfynydd. The man who took his fare and drove the bus watched him with growing curiosity, glancing in his mirror every so often as he tried to settle his mind. At last, pulling up to let an old woman and her daughter climb aboard, he came to the tramp's elbow.

'I seen you somewhere,' he said in Welsh. 'Your face is known to me! I don't want trouble on my bus, see?'

P.C. Williams kept a straight face:

'I won't make trouble, I promise you. I never make trouble, but trouble is my business when it comes.'

The bus driver was uneasy. There were quite a few passengers on the bus and the tramp was being watched by all of them. At last one of them moved and came to sit beside the seemingly outcast passenger.

'Hello, Williams,' he said. 'Been on your holidays?'

The policeman laughed. 'Traws been quiet while I been away?' he asked, and all at once the bus driver knew who he was.

9
Over the Hills to Abergynolwyn

PERSONAL DIARY:

Today was pig-killing time in Abergynolwyn. It was a fine dry day. Pig's liver for my supper.

WHEN they moved over the hills to Abergynolwyn and settled in the greystone village nestling in the bowl of the hills beside the Dysynni River they all brought with them a secret hope that here they might stay a little longer. P.C. Williams looked over the bridge and saw salmon in the pools. He looked at the high hills and the crags and saw the buzzard sailing. Away down the river cormorants were flying and at night he could hear the fox yelping. All the things he had enjoyed elsewhere were here in abundance and the people were kind and friendly, although much better integrated than anywhere he had served before.

'You fish, Mr Williams?' an old man asked him.

He nodded enthusiastically. He enjoyed all the things a country-bred man enjoyed, going up the stream to catch the trout in spring, waiting for the seatrout and the salmon to run late on in summer, catching something for his dinner, the sound of the quiet world in which he lived, the cawing of jackdaws, the cry of the raven. He wasn't always and entirely a policeman, although the world might think of policemen like that. Sometimes the old Occurrence Book was a burden, especially when he had to record the tiresome little things that came day by day after the sergeant had jogged his elbow, having had his own jogged in turn. Why was it so important to record, for instance, riding a bicycle without a light? Anyone who inspected the book could tell that the string of cases didn't mean an epidemic of lawlessness but a purge. Someone would suddenly complain that cattle or sheep were straying on the road and that would be the prime offence for a few weeks, that and driving a motor car without displaying a road fund licence, a rear light, a numberplate. In Abergynolwyn it was much the same as anywhere else. Someone used a beer-bottle label on his motorbike hoping to deceive him and there was an epidemic of wheeling bicycles at night because they knew that the sergeant was always prodding about that offence as the darker evenings began to set in. Then, as sure as the farmers began to cut bracken to bed their cattle, there was salmon poaching. He had been back through the book, reading the hand of his predecessor and a dozen more, all recording the same things: salmon poaching, trespass in pursuit of game and, seemingly for the less adventuresome but equally persistent offender, arrears in bastardy.

In this place, he was told, you must belong to the community and work along with them and they'll be a great help, especially if you close an eye once in a while and pretend not to see something they know well you must have seen. Ignore some of the complaints you get and in a little while you'll belong!

He ignored the complaints about the piggeries, not because he wanted to belong, or because he was particularly partial to the awful smell of pigs but because he didn't see what he could do about it. Pigs and the piggery were an important part of the domestic economy of the little place. Early in the year the small pigs bought by each family would be installed in their sties and fed with everything that could be spared to fatten them. The manure from the pigsties was used in the garden of the family that owned pigs and most families did. At the back end of the year the pigs were slaughtered off and one sold to pay for the food while the other was cured or salted to provide bacon for the family in the following winter. It was an enterprise upon which the pig-owners lavished part of their free time. Inevitably each family became deeply attached to a pair of pigs that grunted and squealed in the communal piggery and contributed to the strong odour which, in high summer, pervaded a good part of the little place.

'I am concerned with offences against the law,' P.C. Williams told an old woman who complained bitterly of the smell and had no pig of her own. 'Pigs can make whatever smell they like, but if they do it is a civil offence!'

'You say that because you get something out of it!'

He looked sternly at her. 'I warn you about making allegations against me as a police officer. Now you go home and forget about the pigs. Get something to occupy your mind!'

Even the most busily-occupied cottager might have found it difficult to forget the pigs in summer. The manure heap grew, the flies busied themselves, the pigs thrived and advertised themselves with squeals and grunts as well as odour. Those who owned them sighed once in a while at the thought of the killing time.

'You never been here at the killing time, Mr Williams?' someone asked him. He had to admit that he hadn't. 'It is a very special time, Mr Williams. You'll be busy that day.'

He forgot all about it until one evening, coming back from the river with a salmon in his hand, he saw sticks, brushwood and kindling being unloaded from a wagon. Mounds of the stuff had been brought to kindle fires on the morrow. Everyone who had a pig also had a cauldron, two cauldrons, it seemed, and beneath each cauldron a fire was laid. The killing time was at hand. The quarry-men were looking forward to some roast ribs, a bit of pork, some fried pig's liver. The children were already claiming the bladders they had been promised months before, although the pigs whose bladders were so coveted for football were still sleepily grunting in their bracken beds.

'There will be a bit of hold-up in Abergynolwyn to-morrow,' said his nearest neighbour, 'and maybe a few arguments and some rough stuff. The squire doesn't care to have so much stuff chopped down for the fires and he doesn't like all the offal being dumped in the river, guts and blood.'

He began to see that the killing time might be one of the great events in the year and it proved to be so.

In the morning he awoke to the smell of woodsmoke. Every quarryman had seen to it that the fire was well alight before going off to his work. The cauldrons sat in the midst of smoke, surrounded by supplies of fuel. It would be several hours before they billowed steam and the water became hot enough for the pig-sticker's purpose, the scalding and cleansing of pig. Small boys hung around and seemed intent upon dodging school that day. The schoolmaster came after them and P.C. Williams herded them in the direction of the school gate, although more than one managed to drift away like a stray dog. They all wanted to see the pig-killer when he arrived on the scene with his armoury of cleavers, sharp knives and steels to keep the edge on the blades of his weapons. He was an enormous man, red-faced, rotund, whiskered. He rode a bicycle upon which all his gear was hung from leather harness slung on the cross-bar. His arrival stopped conversation. It was as though the hangman himself had come to Abergynolwyn. The village stood in awe of him this day. On any other day he might have come through from Towyn with hardly a glance in his direction but today Abergynolwyn was full of drama. The atmosphere seemed to have infected the condemned pigs although their clamour may have been to some extent due to the fact that on the killing day they had gone without their mash, their swill and titbits. Who, after all, would feed a pig when even a hundredweight of mash wouldn't improve its dead weight by as much as an ounce. No one wept for the pig in the morning. The weeping time came later. First the executioner had to have his hour. He rode into the middle of the village, conscious of his importance, aware that he was a person held in awe by the entire community. He set his heavy bicycle against the wall, took off his jacket and put on his leather apron. They stood back from him as though they didn't know him. He gave them good morning in Welsh and looked up at the sky. P.C. Williams watched a scene of growing tension and heard the gasp as the pig-sticker lifted one of his knives and tested it on a hair which he held between finger and thumb. Having done this the killer pushed back his greasy cap and strode to the first piggery.

'Who is first today?' he demanded, looking into the double piggery. Neither wanted to be first. The pig-sticker looked round, fingering a twist of rope and a short stick which he would use hauling up his first victim.

'I haven't got all bloody day!' he shouted.

P.C. Williams moved uneasily, wondering if shortly he would have to assert himself to reassure the community, but a timid woman came forward and gave her assent to the killing before she retreated again, pale, anxious, her apron being wrung in her hands.

The pig-sticker quickly secured the pig.

'A little help, Policeman!' he grunted as the pig, one

of the fattest in the piggery, struggled and fought to escape the hand of doom.

P.C. Williams put his knee against the pig's flank. In a minute the poor animal was in the grip of its executioner. The knife went in, blood began to spurt. The hills around echoed to the poor creature's anguished squealing. Small boys materialized from the back entries. Women turned away. The butchered pig was beyond repeal of sentence. Already it seemed to have the pale appearance of pork. Soon it would be disembowelled, shaved of its bristles, cut down with the cleaver, hung in portions, while the second pig squealed as its life blood gushed out with each convulsive kick of its legs. In the background women and children began to cry. They were steadily becoming redder of eye with every minute they watched the slaughter. Smoke made matters worse. Even P.C. Williams brushed tears from his eyes and coughed for smoke was getting into his lungs.

In the meantime a minor problem had arisen. Two lorries and an old car blocked the street in one direction, and a cattle transport and a horse and cart in the other, none of them able to pass because of the crowd of reluctant but fascinated sightseers.

'Get back there!' ordered P.C. Williams. 'Give this fellow room to get through.'

Someone, eager to be rid of the entrails of a pig, was angling through the crowd with a bath brimming with blood and guts destined for the river. No one seemed to consider that the skins might have made sausages, although little else save the grunt of the pig would be wasted. A man in the crowd complained that his feet had been soiled with the contents of the tin bath. There was some pushing and arguing before P.C. Williams could clear the conjested traffic.

'Now look,' he pleaded. 'Can't you wait to get rid of that when it's quieter?'

The man with the bath grinned at him. 'It will never be quieter, Policeman Williams. This will go on all day until it is dark and the river will take it all away sooner if it doesn't all get poured in at once.'

He didn't know what to say. The shrieking of pigs awaiting death joined with the fearful squeals of the animal newly-knifed, and the background hubbub was more than the exchanges of bystanders. It was the sound of human anguish at the loss of a family pet. Everyone, it seemed, had a pig to be killed but no one was quite able to face the prospect of the pig's being executed before their eyes, no one except the pig-sticker and he in his time had killed ten thousand, if not with the jawbone of an ass, with his long sharp knife. There was no other way. Everyone knew that good pork could only be had when the pig was drained of blood, quickly and completely, while its heart assisted in the pumping out of its system.

'It makes me sick,' Arthur confided to his wife when he closed the door on the village at noon and sat down to eat his dinner.

'I never saw so many women crying, even at the war memorial,' said Mary Ellen. 'Why they keep pigs when they get so fond of them, I don't know. Some of them could hardly bring themselves to tell the pig-killer to do what he had to do.'

At that moment there was a loud knocking on the door. P.C. Williams wiped his mouth and went to see who needed him. A quarryman, a little red-haired man, stood looking angrily at him.

'Right then, Williams,' he said. 'You got to come and sort this out for me! I won't have it! Got no right to do it!'

P.C. Williams reached for his notebook and pencil:

'You better tell me what you're talking about. You got a complaint to make you better make it!'

'My name is Harry Hughes. I got a pig. It's been killed! I didn't want it killed. I gave no permission for it to be killed and it's been slaughtered. Anybody will tell you it is my pig and everybody seen it killed!'

'Hold on, hold on, I can't see a man killing your pig without you giving permission.'

The little man danced with rage. 'You don't see! You don't see! I tell you it has been done and everybody seen it!'

P.C. Williams put on his helmet and stepped out into the street. The scene was as busy as ever. The pig-sticker, it seemed, hardly paused in his stride and half the village was occupied already, cutting up pigs that had suddenly ceased to be pets and had become scalded sides of pork or potential shoulders and hams to be salted.

'This man says you killed his pig,' he said to the bloody fellow in the leather apron.

The pig-sticker hesitated and looked over his shoulder:

'That I did. I killed his pig and it's hanging there in his garden. I expect to be paid for it, like everybody else pays. I never do nothing for nothing.'

'It isn't whether you'll get paid or not but whether you lawfully killed his pig, see? I got a complaint that you killed his pig—'

'Every year you'll get a complaint that I kill his pig! Listen, Policeman, every year he tells his wife to see the pig is killed. Every year while he's working in the quarry he changes his mind, thinks he'll get a better price for the pig at Christmas or something like that, and tries to make out I killed his pig without his permission. His wife gives permission and I do what I contract to do. If he's got any complaint it's against his wife.'

P.C. Williams rubbed his nose and looked from one to the other. He had a policeman's instinct for the truth. It was quite plain that the pig-sticker had only done what he was asked to do.

'You better settle this with your missis, Hughes,' he advised, 'instead of shouting and running to my door. I can do nothing about it. Now close your mouth and give yourself time to think!'

'One thing he's got to do is pay me before I leave here!' said the pig-sticker. 'I had bother with him last year!'

P.C. Williams returned to his dinner. He had had enough of things in Abergynolwyn on pig-killing day, but having enough was one thing and being at the end of the day was another. The school came out early. Even the schoolmaster had an interest, a share in a pig, and he had things to do. Small boys ran about with blood-streaked bladders which they tried to inflate before they were dry enough to be inflated. There were fights over the cherished trophies and minor accidents. One child ran crying that his jersey was on fire—it smouldered with a spark from one of the fires—and a woman scalded her hand. P.C. Williams stood by talking and watching the proceedings. He had only just discovered that he, too, was involved in a personal way. There were certain perks for the policeman, things like sweetbreads and trotters which were always set on one side for him. Here and there he might be even more favoured and receive a plate of liver, but none of these things came his way early in the day, only at evening, at dusk when neighbours need run no risk of openly showing favour to the representative of the law. The afternoon wore on with renewed squeals and more weeping and wailing as another family pet, and then another much-loved if somewhat dirty pig, was put to death.

'I never knew anything like this in my life,' said Mary Ellen. 'It must be like this in Africa . . .'

She had read somewhere about African village feasts and tribal rituals and it needed no great stretch of imagination to compare the two.

In the evening a time came when a strange hush fell upon the village. The squealing was over, the fires began to die out under the cauldrons although a pall of smoke hung in the air above the place. The pigs were all slaughtered. Only the shrill cries of boys playing echoed from the hills. P.C. Williams received a plate of trotters at the back door and told Mary Ellen that he couldn't do this kind of thing. He would take himself off down the road. If anyone wanted to give them a bit of pig they could give it to her. It was against regulations. What would the Chief Constable say?

With eight children Mary Ellen hardly cared what the Chief Constable would say! She looked at the trotters and decided that they would make more than one meal and a good pot of soup. No one as hard pressed for money as she was looked a gift pig in the mouth.

Down the road P.C. Williams watched the pig-sticker wiping his knives and cleavers and putting them away on his harness. There was no lamp on his bicycle and all at once the policeman remembered being told by the sergeant that the pig-sticker, Twm Twrch they called him, was a persistent offender. When he came to Abergynolwyn he would ride back to Towyn without a light. He was to be booked.

'You got a light for that bike?' he asked, knowing that Twm Twrch had no light.

The pig-sticker looked at him. 'You can see I haven't, can't you, but you can't do nothing about that, can you? I got to be riding it after lighting-up time, teh?'

And that was true. The sergeant would want to know if he had checked up on Twm Twrch on the road home. There was nothing else for it but to get on his own bicycle and ride down the road to wait in ambush. It was a tiresome thing to do at the end of a trying day, but there was no help for it. He went back to the police station and got out his bicycle, being careful to see that the carbide lamp was burning before he set off. He had hardly gone five yards when he was hailed by someone who hurried out to intercept him.

'Williams, I want you!'

It was Harry Hughes again.

'Look Hughes,' he said, 'I told you before, this isn't something I can do anything about. You haven't got a complaint if you gave your wife authority to have the pig killed!'

'Not that, not that, Williams! The pig has been stolen!'

All at once Williams wanted to laugh, but he smothered the smile that spread across his face. The pig had been stolen! A full-sized pig. Who in Abergynolwyn needed to steal a pig on this particular day? Who could carry a pig as far as it needed to be carried? It was undoubtedly in some near-by shed or outhouse, but a search would have to be made and it was already almost dark.

'I'll come and take a statement from you,' he said, not keen to have the aggressive little fellow in the police station at that particular time. 'I expect somebody has played a joke on you . . .'

The statement was a formality. Mrs Hughes butted in several times to say that the pig, dressed out in two sides, had been hanging in the porch and now it was gone. She had seen it with her own eyes. Harry Hughes had seen it when he had washed the quarry dust off himself at half-past five. Carefully P.C. Williams studied the ground round the porch by the light of his bicycle lamp. He saw the large footprint on the soft earth and smiled to himself. He had solved the crime, but he said nothing. He must earn himself a certain credit. The pig probably wasn't stolen, but just where it was he had yet to find out. The man to tell him was not so far away, down the street.

'Well, Hughes, that's all for now. I'll be back to see you in a little while, maybe an hour, see?'

'You suspect somebody?'

'Have you anybody in mind yourself?'

Harry Hughes could think of a dozen enemies. He wasn't by any means the most popular villager in Abergynolwyn.

'Leave it to me,' said the policeman. 'Say nothing and leave it all to me. You'll say too much if you're not careful. I'll get your pig back, I think.'

He put his lamp back on the bicycle and rode off down the road towards Towyn, thinking of the road junction where he might waylay the pig-sticker, Twm Twrch. Twm Twrch was still in the village, fortifying himself with a glass of ale or two. Killing was a thirst-provoking business. He was fat enough by any standard, but he had lost weight toiling by the boiling pots. He had earned more than the fees he had collected!

At the road junction P.C. Williams put out his own lights and pushed the bicycle into the hedge. It wasn't an unpleasant vigil. The moon came up and its light fell on the woods and slopes of the valley, leaving the face of Bird Rock in shadow. He could smell the mouldering leaves, the decay of autumn and woodsmoke on the breeze. When he got back home Mary Ellen would have a pork chop for his supper and maybe a bit of liver.

Twm Twrch was a long time coming. By the time he appeared, a bulky figure wobbling along on the moonlit ribbon of straight road, P.C. Williams was glad to see him. He rose up and prepared himself for the ambush. But he had reckoned without the crafty mind of Twm Twrch, who had run into an ambush more than once before on this very stretch of road. While almost a hundred yards still separated them Twm Twrch swung his leg over the seat of his bicycle and came to a clattering halt on the road. Thereafter he walked steadily and relentlessly forward, his armoury rattling against the frame of his unlit bicycle.

'All right, Twm Twrch,' said the disappointed policeman. 'All right, but how long you been walking?'

Twm Twrch scratched his fat chin and peered up at the moon:

'Since I was about three years old, my mother tells me, Policeman. Maybe longer. I don't know.'

There was no help for it. The sergeant would have to be told that the ambush hadn't worked. It didn't really amount to much. A five-shilling fine. There would be other days in other places.

'Well,' said Twm Twrch, 'I got to be on my way.'

'Not so fast, not so fast. I got a few questions to ask you Mr Twrch. To begin with did you get your money from Harry Hughes?'

'I never get my money from Harry Hughes until I go there and threaten to cut his throat! Harry Hughes and money are like pig's blood running into the river, you can't separate them!'

'And Harry Hughes has lost the pig you killed for him. . .'

'Indeed, indeed. There's hard luck for you, teh?'

'Very hard luck. Now I been on the scene of the crime,' said the policeman, 'and there on the soil by the porch I took note of a footprint of a boot.'

Twm Twrch nodded and scratched his chin again.

'And the nails in that boot had a certain pattern, Mr Twrch, which I took note of. Now I got to eliminate certain people from this suspicion I have, so if you'll be good enough to let me see the kind of boots you've got on your feet. . .'

Even in the moonlight it was impossible to see the nails in the sole of the boot that Twm Twrch cocked up for inspection. P.C. Williams fumbled for a match and struck it, but the breeze blew it out again.

'You're not having a lot of luck, Policeman, are you?' asked Twm Twrch.

'You'd be surprised how lucky I can be,' he said. 'You might be surprised how lucky you are too, for I have a complaint and not just the size of the footprints at the scene of the crime match your boots but the nail pattern!'

A second match confirmed his suspicion but he knew very well that the pig-sticker would have a ready explanation.

'I expect I carried the pig to his porch,' said Twm Twrch. 'I'm that kind of man, see? Even when I'm dealing with a skinflint like Harry Hughes—'

'And Harry Hughes testifies that he carried the pig to his own porch in his dinner hour soon after he came to complain that you had killed it—'

'The porch is a bad place to hang a pig newly killed, too close and stuffy like . . . I moved it for him, see?'

P.C. Williams had come up against frustration of this kind many times before. There was nothing on the book. There would be nothing on the book, no crime reported, no crime unsolved, so long as Harry Hughes got his pig back.

'Where is it then?'

'Hanging in a tree down beside the river. I thought it would cool better there, see? I wasn't happy about it in that old porch of his.'

'I hope it's still there, Mr Twrch. You admit you moved it from his porch? There might be a complaint yet because you moved it without his permission, you took it away and put it somewhere else. You've heard of intent to steal? You know that taking something away is stealing if you haven't the owner's consent?'

The pig-sticker seemed deflated. 'I was only getting my own back on him, Policeman. I wasn't stealing his bloody pig.'

'Then we'll say you'll hear no more about it if I get the pig back; and one more thing, when you come this way again you'll have a light on that bike, teh? You won't have me running after you, big man though you are? You were very full of yourself in Abergynolwyn today.

Fair play, it's a big day, but Abergynolwyn is my beat, my patch and anybody that takes liberties there makes more work for me catching fools who imitate him, so next time you come you come with a light!'

'The pig is in the tree, the big old ash tree on this side of the river,' said Twm Twrch.

P.C. Williams bade him goodnight and rode back up the moonlit road whistling to himself. He had put Twm Twrch in his place and found the pig and there was no laborious writing to be done in the Occurrence Book!

'Hughes,' he said when the little quarryman answered the door in response to his knock, 'as a result of certain information which I have managed to uncover, I think I can take you to the place where your missing pig is to be found. Bring a lamp.'

Harry Hughes dutifully found a storm lantern, although in the street the bright moonlight hardly made the lamp necessary. Down along the river in the shadows of the trees and bushes they were glad of the lamp, however, and at last they came upon the two sides of pig, hoisted high on a stout branch, the end of which Twm Twrch had lopped off with one of his razor-sharp cleavers.

'Only a very big strong man could have put it there,' said Harry Hughes. 'Twm Twrch!'

P.C. Williams began to think of all the complications pursuit of such a line would involve.

'Hughes,' he said, 'don't push things too hard, will you?'

The little man almost fell over under the weight of the two sides of pig which dropped upon him as the tall policeman cut the cord holding them on the branch. He got up, floundered again and allowed himself to be raised to his feet. P.C. Williams relieved him of half his burden and carried a side of pig up the field to the road.

'You might not have got your pig back at all but for me! You've no real evidence against Twm Twrch. It might have been some tramp. In the morning the pig might have been gone from the tree. Think about it. You're a lucky man, Harry Hughes, and if I were in your shoes I'd pay Twm Twrch his money before very long.'

Harry Hughes grunted like a pig and said nothing, but P.C. Williams was content. He went back to the police station and put away his bicycle.

'I got a nice bit of fried liver for you,' said Mary Ellen.

He sat down and ate it thinking about all that had happened. He was glad that the killing time came only once a year to Abergynolwyn. It turned the place upside-down. People were not themselves for a day but disturbed by emotion, love, hate, rage. In the morning the pools of the river would have pigs' entrails in them and the rats would scavenge in among the stones there along with hens, crows, seagulls and half-starved dogs.

10

The Pursuit of Poachers

EVIDENCE IN COURT:

"I asked him to lend me his bicycle pump. On taking the pump I discovered that the interior had been done away with and the pump case used to carry limed sticks with which the defendant admitted he had set out to catch goldfinches.'

EARLY in the year, soon after his first winter in Abergynolwyn, P.C. Williams bought an aviary. Mary Ellen watched him bring it home with a certain degree of amazement mixed with horror; for it was a sizable structure and it arrived perched on top of a lorry, to be dismantled at the front door, transported through the house and upstairs, and there reassembled, a feat not without difficulty considering that the aviary had not been designed for incorporation in a dwelling house! It was an outdoor structure, but this fact didn't daunt the policeman. He had his aviary reconstructed in the upper part of the police station in no time, and only the merry singing of his birds betrayed their presence to his superiors.

'Do I hear birds singing, Williams?' asked the inspector.

'In the garden, sir,' he said. 'I'll open the window and you'll hear them better.'

This was true. The window of the room housing the aviary was open and the inspector would hear the birds a great deal better with the downstairs window open too. P.C. Williams wasn't exactly sure that his superiors would give their blessing to the property of the Constabulary being used for such a purpose. Mary Ellen wasn't sure either. The seed and water had mingled on the floor and, in the compost of droppings and grit, a fine crop of hay had begun to sprout from the floorboards.

It was P.C. Williams's interest in birds that had drawn his attention to the character known as Will Snatcher, who troubled the water bailiff in and out of season. For Will Snatcher, a highly-skilled salmon poacher, was also a catcher of birds, birds of all sorts, from a fat cock pheasant to a pretty-as-paint goldfinch settling on teazle or Scotch thistle.

'I'll have you one day, Snatcher,' Williams warned, but the cunning of Will Snatcher was highly developed. He had never been taken for bird-catching and somehow or other he managed to survive the blows of fate when he happened to be caught red-handed, at work on the river.

'I don't mind a salmon or two,' P.C. Williams confided to Mary Ellen. 'Salmon is food. I wouldn't bother very much about his pheasants except that the old squire gives me half-a-crown for chasing him, but I got no time for bird-catchers! I like to see goldfinches singing on the tree. I don't like to think of them being sold off in Liverpool or Wrexham, or somewhere like that, and smashing themselves against the bars of a little wire cage. For that, and his dirty game with lime, I'd like to see Will Snatcher go to prison!'

It wasn't often that her husband was so vehement in his condemnation of a law-breaker. Live and let live was part of his code. Not everyone who offended against the law was prosecuted, although most were reminded, one way or another, of their wrong-doing and mended their ways. Will Snatcher had a certain defiance about the way he did things. Everyone knew he took more salmon than his family could eat, more pheasants too, and all kinds of birds, from bullfinches and goldfinches to linnets and buntings. With one thing and another he no longer worked in the quarry.

Things were not always in Will Snatcher's favour, however. The day he taunted the bailiff from the far bank of the swollen river he hardly expected that individual to recruit the aid of the policeman, for he knew that the policeman was rarely eager to co-operate with the bailiff. The bailiff, however, had decided that the time had come to bring Will Snatcher before the bench once again, and to do that he had to have P.C. Williams on his side or, to be more accurate, on the opposite side of the river.

'Mrs Williams,' he said, when he reached the village and knocked on the police station door, 'I got to have help quick. Where is Policeman Williams?'

Mary Ellen frowned and went upstairs. P.C. Williams was studying his birds again.

'If you can bring yourself to forget the birds,' she said, frowning at the verdure on the floor, 'you might attend to Price. He says he needs your help urgently. I think he's after that Will Snatcher again.'

P.C. Williams sighed and dusted the seed husks and feathers from his knees. Duty was duty no matter when he was called. For a village policeman there was no whistle-blowing, no time to go out and no time to come back.

'All right,' he said. 'If he wants to catch Will Snatcher we'll catch him, but I'd just as soon hold his head under water for half an hour. That'd cure his poaching.'

Price the bailiff was almost dancing with anxiety to be off and catch Will Snatcher. P.C. Williams buttoned his tunic, put on his helmet and prepared himself for the road without hurrying too much.

'How far up has he gone?' he asked.

Price shook his head. He didn't know how many salmon there were in the pools, but he knew that Will Snatcher would know, and he had had a sack with him. By now he would have at least two, or maybe three fish.

'I'll ride up the road and come down. You stay below the stepping stones, then if he comes down ahead of me you can slip across and nab him.'

Price was satisfied that they would take their man. He watched the policeman ride off. It was a fine morning for the business. Late-run fish were still on the way, a fact that Will Snatcher knew only too well. He had orders for them from hotelkeepers, who never reminded him that there was a season for all things, and salmon were protected at certain times.

On the way down the river P.C. Williams stopped and watched a fish hanging in a deep pool. He could have taken it himself had he come armed with a hook or a gaff. It would have fed his family for a week. Will Snatcher had nine children, one more than the policeman had, although the numbers would soon be balanced, nine-all, when another son was born. It wasn't the fish, it was the birds that really mattered, the policeman told himself. One day, instead of helping the water bailiff look after fish that belonged to his boss, he would catch Will Snatcher robbing everybody, taking the birds that sang on the hedge or the wall, a far greater crime. At that moment, looking down the bank, he saw the long gaff come out from the bushes, like the arm of a thief, and a second or two later the water boiled and frothed as a salmon, neatly snatched, fought for all it was worth to get free. The crime had been witnessed but the poacher was out of sight. What was equally important was that the snatched fish was now also out of sight, and Will Snatcher had to be taken with the tools of his trade and evidence of their having been used. He jumped up the bank and pounded along to catch the snatcher. Will Snatcher had no time to throw the gaff away. He was still unravelling the iron head from its staff. The salmon lay at his feet but it wasn't there for long. He kicked it and it began to slide down the bank and into the water. P.C. Williams dived for it and tripped over the gaff but his outstretched hand closed on the 'wrist' of the salmon's tail.

Will Snatcher stared at him for a moment.

'I found them on the bank,' he said. 'Somebody must have been snatchin', teh?'

'Somebody like yourself,' said the policeman. 'I got all I need, the fish, your snatching tool, and you! I got a complaint that you had gone up the river. You might as well admit it.'

'Admit nothin',' said Will Snatcher. 'Nothin'!'

It hardly mattered. P.C. Williams marched his prisoner all the way down river, with Price in tow carrying the gaff, the sack and the fish.

'Illegal fishing in private waters,' said P.C. Williams. 'Snatching. Do you deny that this gaff is your property? That you were apprehended in possession of both the gaff and this salmon?'

Will Snatcher said nothing. Charged with his offence he still said nothing. The inspector frowned and said it was typical. Snatcher did not say anything. He didn't make a plea either, until the very last minute and that by letter. P.C. Williams sighed and felt a little sorry for Price. He could never win! On the day of the court both he and Price would have to make the journey to give evidence against Will Snatcher, should he plead not guilty, but Will Snatcher would plead guilty—by letter —and stay at home awaiting his fine, or at least preparing to pay his fine by catching as many fish from the pools as he could—on a day when he knew quite well both the policeman and the bailiff were far away! There was no help for it, and in due course Will Snatcher again paid his fine and made a nice profit.

'Wait until the summer,' said P.C. Williams. 'Wait and I'll have him for putting out lime for goldfinches. . .'

Late in the summer when the finches were beginning to fly in company, sailing over from one thistle field to another, and filling the sunlit afternoon with their tinkling music, P.C. Williams watched and waited for Will Snatcher. There was no sign of bird-catching gear, however. Many a time the policeman rode a long way over the hills on the trail of the bird-catcher, only to find that the journey was futile. And then one afternoon, just as he was deciding to let Will Snatcher ride out alone, an old fellow sidled up to him:

'Don't go when he goes! Wait a while and ride along the road to the field beside the bridge. You'll find him there. He puts the birds in a bag inside his jacket and the lime sticks are in his bicycle pump, which is only a shell and not a proper pump at all!'

Even a village policeman depends mainly on informants, titbits of information, bits of gossip, a word or two here and there that may lead to an offender being caught. All at once P.C. Williams understood why he had failed. His shadowing might or might not have been close. Will Snatcher might on one occasion have had no chance to put out his limed sticks, but how many times, depending on the policeman being far enough behind, had he slipped over a gate and put his sticks among the thistles and come back again to collect his birds and return the limed sticks to the inside of the bicycle pump?

'I'll have you now, Will Snatcher,' he promised. 'To-day, tomorrow, the next day.'

Will Snatcher would have been more careful had he known that his subterfuge was no longer effective. The next day, when he was about to jump on his bicycle and ride away from a field gate, he was startled to find the policeman at his elbow, gently bringing him to a halt and feeling under the flapping tails of his old jacket.

'Goldfinches, Snatcher. . .'

'I found the poor little beggars in that field. Somebody had put down birdlime, see? I was taking them home to clean them. . .'

'Lend me your pump, my tyre's flat,' said the policeman. 'We'll ride together. You can tell me all about it at the police station, eh?'

Will Snatcher looked at the pump and then at the policeman.

'How did you know, Williams?' he asked.

'A little bird told me, Snatcher!'

They went down the road side by side, P.C. Williams carrying the pump and the black bag of limed goldfinches.

'You'll be fined for each one, I reckon,' said the policeman. 'I hope they throw the book at you!'

When in due course the inspector took over the prosecution he read what the constable had written.

'Smart work, Williams,' he said. 'What about the birds?'

'I cleaned them up, sir,' he said, 'and let them go, all except three that were smothered and died. I wish I could have smothered Will Snatcher. I'm very fond of birds.'

'That fact has already been reported, Williams. The Chief is not so very fond of them, so maybe you better move that lot upstairs before he comes round! The sergeant told you, I suppose, that he's having a personal tour of inspection of police houses tomorrow afternoon?'

P.C. Williams's mouth fell open. He looked at the inspector in dismay.

'What will I do, sir?' he asked.

'Get them out, Williams, get them out! No other thing you can do, unless you want to be thrown out of the Force.'

P.C. Williams waited until the inspector had gone and rushed through to Mary Ellen.

'I've got to get all the birds out! The Chief Constable is coming to inspect the house tomorrow! What can I do?'

'Let them go,' said Mary Ellen, enjoying herself for a moment. 'Cut all that grass you've been growing up there, stop treading seeds and feathers all over my clean house!'

The downcast Arthur sat on the bottom step of the stairs and was in despair. After a while he recovered and began considering how he could cope with his problem in the time available. There was an empty house next door. It belonged to an old lady at the other end of the village. He would go and see her and get permission to move the aviary into her empty house, at least for the period while the Chief Constable would be in the district.

'You can use the room for a day or two,' he was told. 'But no longer. I got a tenant coming on Friday, see?'

Thankfully he promised to be away by Friday. The operation of catching up his fifty or sixty birds, caging them, stripping the wooden aviary, taking it downstairs, out of the house, and along to the next house where it was reassembled, took him all afternoon, all evening and all morning. At three o'clock the following afternoon he swept away the last vestige of seed and looked into a room he felt the Chief Constable would pass as suitable. At four o'clock he had his books laid out for inspection and everything in the office straight and as tidy as it would have been for H.M. Inspector of Constabulary in person, but the Chief Constable didn't come! At eight o'clock in the evening P.C. Williams knew the Chief wasn't coming. By mid-day the following day he knew that the Chief would never come, and he began moving the aviary and the birds back again. A day later everything was as it had been, and the inspector arrived unexpectedly.

'Williams,' he said, 'I thought I told you the Chief Constable didn't like birds?'

'You did, sir.'

'And I advised you to get them out of there?'

'And I did, sir.'

'And you brought them back, Williams. That was rash, wasn't it Williams, because the Chief had to put off his inspection for two days? He'll be here tomorrow. Now in your shoes I'd get rid of those birds, eh?'

The constable groaned. He couldn't think of all that had to be done without wishing himself dead!

'I don't know what to do now, sir,' he said. 'I haven't the strength to tackle it all again, sir—'

The inspector's face broke into a grin. 'Keep your chin up, Williams! I been listening to a little bird too. It tells me the Chief Constable's gone for a holiday in South Wales! I go in and put seed in a little dish for his pet canary, see?'

There isn't very much a mere constable can say to an inspector in such circumstances. P.C. Williams said nothing. His birds were still singing away happily when Will Snatcher was fined, or given the option of going to prison for catching wild birds by the use of birdlime.

Hardly had the autumn arrived than the squire called, seeking his co-operation in catching poachers from Abergynolwyn who were after his birds. Abergynolwyn lacked nothing in the way of talent in this direction. It boasted men who were as adept at snaring a pheasant as they were at snatching a salmon. Quarry work had always been irregular, depending on the market for slates, the weather, and so on; and next to quarrying, poaching was perhaps the most important trade followed by those not in regular employment.

'Catch me two or three, Williams,' said the squire, 'and I'll bear you in mind. I'll speak to the Chief Constable when I see him.'

P.C. Williams stood in awe of the Chief Constable, like most everyday village policemen, but he knew what the squire meant. The Chief Constable might not be told about his diligence over poaching, but about his failure to do as the squire wanted.

'Do my best, sir,' he said.

'Good man, Williams. Get them on the run. Put a stop to their game. That's all I ask!'

Justice is seen to be done and everyone is happy. Catching the men who went after the squire's pheasants involved the policeman in long vigils that came to nothing, but he contrived to make sure that the squire saw that he was keeping an eye open, even chasing those who might be trespassing in pursuit of game. More than once, knowing that the old autocrat was riding in a certain direction P.C. Williams put his bicycle in the hedge and waited until the squire was in his immediate locality before making a dash after imaginary poachers who, because of his lack of breath and staying power just managed to escape! He would return to the road, panting and gasping and step into the path of the squire remarking, 'They just managed to get away, sir. They had a good start on me, I'm sorry to say!' The squire's pleasure would shine on his florid countenance. 'Well done, Williams! Well done! Next time if you think I'm at hand give a shout. I'll ride after them and maybe between us we'll nail them!' Such devotion to duty had to be rewarded, as the policeman well knew. The squire invariably dipped into his pocket and produced half-a-crown. It was worth the dash across a field or along the back of a wood. The poachers sat in the public house in Abergynolwyn drinking their pints of beer. A man had to make a living one way or another. They had their way and the policeman, who wasn't a bad fellow, had his. Once in a while their paths crossed and once in a while he got his hand on their collars. They expected no mercy and they got none. It was all very well running but once in a while someone had to be caught.

The pursuit of game was a crime in itself but the magistrates were inclined to take more notice of evidence a little more tangible than a wire noose or even an old hammer-gun and a cartridge. Some of the poachers told extraordinary tales to justify their unlawful presence on farmland or in woods. They would claim that they had been given permission by the tenant, that they had gone to destroy rabbits at his request, that they had had permission from the tenant's father or even his grand-father, that they weren't pursuing game or conies but shooting moles! A brace of pheasants was the evidence that the prosecutor liked best, game to show the bench and, when the case was concluded, a reasonable list of previous convictions.

The well-organized poacher would hide his game in a wood or behind a hedge, dismantle his gun and take it home in the lining of his ragged coat, and it was hard to bring the offender to book without either catching him in the woods in the act of shooting or taking him with the game he had killed. P.C. Williams had found himself in so many situations where mere courage and strength were not enough and soon he decided that what he really needed was a dog. The inspector scratched his head and said he had better make sure that the dog did no harm to anyone charged with an offence or the Chief would be sending for him. The big black Alsatian dog was probably one of the first police dogs used in Wales. Certainly it was an untrained animal, but its presence at the police-man's heels was enough to put thoughts of violence from the mind of any tinker, vagrant or poacher the constable happened to encounter by day or by night. The Alsatian had a good nose and with a little assistance from its master who had suspicions about the places in which poachers might have left the game they hoped to sell, pheasants were now and again located and watched over. The result of keeping observation on a brace of dead birds wasn't always a conviction, but Mary Ellen was pleased when, at last deciding that the poacher had no intention of returning for the birds. P.C. Williams brought them home.

'Here,' he would say, 'get them ready for the oven, eh? If they lie there any longer they'll get maggoty or a rat will start on them and we might as well have a dinner out of it. I've earned it sitting in the hedge watching, haven't I?'

This kind of bonus came his way every so often. The inspector was aware of time spent by the policeman keeping in the squire's good books.

'One day somebody will have to tell him he's no more than any other member of the public,' he said. 'Game keeping is a job for gamekeepers and while you're earning yourself a pheasant somebody might be stealing the money from one of the shops in the village, eh?'

P.C. Williams enjoyed eating the evidence far more than going through the tiresome rigmarole of bringing a talkative, plausible rogue before the bench. Welsh magistrates have always been noted for their sympathy and leniency towards poachers, in any case, and the truth was that no one except the estate owners considered the offence as anything but a sort of demonstration against privilege.

There was an occasion when, warned of an expedition after pheasants planned by three brothers living in the village, P.C. Williams went forth with his dog in the middle of the night, walking along the grass verge to the wood in which the poachers were operating and resisting the temptation to head in the direction of shots which from time to time echoed in the moonlit thicket. The poachers seemed to be doing well, but then, after he had suddenly had the feeling that he had been observed on the road, the shots ceased and the wood fell silent save for the sound of a cracking twig. His quarry had taken alarm. There was no doubt of that. Now they were either waiting for him, hiding their game, or heading for home and he had to make up his mind. The moon hung in a clear sky by this time. The silence was uncanny. There was no way of telling whether the poachers were lying still or on the move, but after a long time he heard a dog bark away down the road and then, still farther away, another dog barking. It took him a minute or two to understand the meaning of the barking. The three men, walking the grass verge as he had himself done, had passed two sleeping cottages, but the kennelled dogs had heard them. Already he was in danger of being deprived of the fruits of his labour. Tomorrow his informant would ask him what had happened and the three brothers would quietly grin at one another and down their pints in the pub to order more and drink his health. He began to run along the road with his dog at his heels, disregarding the grass verge and not caring whether they heard him coming or not.

It was a pity the squire wasn't there to give him half-a-crown when he came upon the sack lying in the road on the outskirts of the village. He heard a door bang shut and knew that he had failed, but if he could gain admittance there might be evidence that would clinch the matter: muddy boots, a feather or two on a jacket, an uncleaned gun or guns. He swung the sack on his shoulder and hurried to knock on the door. No one answered until his hammering seemed about to break the door down and then at last a man in his shirt tails confronted him.

'What you want?' he demanded.

'You dropped a sack on the road,' he said.

'I dropped nothin'. I don't know what you're talking about.'

The policeman put his foot in the door, tipped up the sack and let the contents spill on to the doorstep. There was more in the sack than five pheasants, for tumbling out came a checked cloth cap, an old, greasy cap that anyone in the village could have identified as being the property of the eldest of the three brothers. The two men stared at it for a moment.

'You put Llew's cap in that sack!'

'I think I better come in and ask Llew where he left his cap,' he replied, pushing his way in. 'You been in bed long?'

The big black Alsatian came in without being asked. It sniffed round the room and tugged at a coat in the pocket of which the policeman discovered a sixth pheasant. Evidently the brothers hadn't waited to put the entire bag of pheasants in their sack.

'I want a word with you, Llew,' said the constable, walking straight through into the bedroom and pulling back the bedclothes. Llew hadn't waited to strip to his shirt. He had got into bed with his trousers on and his muddy boots stuck up to reproach him when he protested that a man had a right to sleep in his bed without being disturbed in the middle of the night.

'All of you up and along to the police station,' said P.C. Williams. 'I'll wait for you and take charge of these guns.'

He found one of the guns still loaded and cocked. The three brothers looked at one another in the moonlight and he could tell the sort of telepathic message that was passing from one to the other.

'Boys,' he said tersely, 'that dog is very jealous. Won't let my wife touch me.'

The big black dog looked up at him, sensing his alarm perhaps, for the hairs on its neck rose in a thick ruff and the rumble of a growl sounded deep in its chest.

'I don't think I could hold him off if he attacked somebody attacking me,' said P.C. Williams. 'I wouldn't like to try. He could tear a man's throat out.'

The three poachers said nothing. Gingerly the one who had been shivering in his shirt tails began putting on his trousers. The other two were already sufficiently clothed to step out on to the road. P.C. Williams lifted the pheasants and the checked cap and put them back into the sack.

At the police station he put the guns in the corner of the office, tipped out the contents of the sack and stepped behind his table.

'Right then,' he said, 'I warn you that you will be charged with offences under the Night Poaching Act and anything you may say will be taken down by me and may be used in evidence. You understand what I am telling you?'

They understood. They had been in the same situation before but rarely with so much damning evidence on the record.

'You and your bloody dog, Williams,' said the youngest. 'I could have shot you on the road—'

P.C. Williams stood up. 'Now look my lad, I'm going to see you go for poaching, see? What you have just said could be made into something very much more serious. . . I've a book full of charges here on my table. Poaching pheasants is the one I want and I'll be satisfied with that if you behave yourself. . .'

'All right, Williams,' said the owner of the checked cap, 'he never said he would have shot you. He never shot you, but you hunted us with a dog, didn't you?'

'I take my dog for a walk every night, Llew,' he said grimly.

The inspector was pleased with his night's work when he read over the statements.

'That cap was a bit of luck and finding a pheasant inside the cottage was a Godsend, teh?' he said. 'But I wonder they didn't set about you when you went in. They could have thrown you and the pheasant out on the road and you'd have had a job making it stick without a witness.'

P.C. Williams smiled to himself. He had been aware of the danger and the difficulties from the outset.

'I had the dog, sir,' he said. 'A dog is a very useful animal when it comes to trouble of this kind. My dog watches all the time. They couldn't have lifted a finger. He'd have had one of them.'

The magistrates looked at the evidence which, by the time it was tipped out for inspection, was a little high and rather tattered and dishevelled. The three brothers were awarded a month in prison.

This time P.C. Williams didn't eat the evidence. It was too high.

II

Water Under the Bridge

IMAGINARY CHARGE:

That you, Police Constable Arthur Howell Williams, Number Twenty-one, Merioneth Constabulary, did unlawfully and wilfully take a quantity of fish, valued at 10s from Bryn Teg Lake on Monday July 27th last, such waters being private property of Mrs Lloyd Thomas, Bryn Teg Estate.

BY the time their ninth and last child was born (christened Reginald Kenneth Williams in 1929) P.C. Williams and his wife had settled comfortably into the life of Abergynolwyn where, in due course, he was to serve out the remainder of his regular Police career. Here he would become not merely the counsellor of the village in things apertaining to the law, but the right-hand man of the Vicar, who discovered in him the material he had been seeking in a warden. He would play the organ on Sunday and his youngest son would work the bellows handle. He would be all things to all men, an official of the Legion, an encouragement to the founders of the angling society, a stalwart of the St John Ambulance Brigade. There would be no promotion. He had never sought it. He had never wanted stripes on his sleeve like his brother, or his father, although he was proud of himself in his 'dress' uniform, a specially smart tunic, belt and other accoutrements which members of the Merioneth Constabulary were required to wear when the circuit judge visited the county town of Dolgellau. When the assizes were held constables in outlying places looked forward to being drafted into the county town. There they paraded, spick and span and splendid, in their ceremonial attire, as proud as peacocks and revelling in the glamour, such as there was, in Dolgellau, and enjoying the good ale. Preparing for the Judge's Javelin, as it was called, P.C. Williams was concerned to see that no one could find fault with his turn-out. His belt had to shine like patent leather. His boots were boned by Mary Ellen until she could see her face in them. His tunic was sponged and pressed and examined for stains or signs of moth. He stood as straight as a round rush, although he was no longer the fresh-faced country lad whose picture Mary Ellen had admired in the printer's window in Accrington.

'Am I all right?' he would ask her, slipping his helmet strap under his chin and looking to his front. Mary Ellen would walk round him as though he were a monument in Dolgellau and assure him that he was fit to be seen and inspected by the Chief Constable—or the most exalted of H.M.'s Judges, gowned, bewigged and himself full of ritual and ceremonial!

Thus assured, P.C. Williams would take himself off without a single qualm about leaving Abergynolwyn to its own resources for a day or two. He knew that whatever happened it wouldn't take him long to get to the bottom of it on his return. Anyone who committed a serious offence would be dealt with by officers up from Towyn or some other corner, but the day-to-day crimes of the men and boys of the village would be answered for on the return of their own constable. Woe betide anyone who tried to get away with anything during this short holiday when he was in the company of men he met only once a year.

'You must wait until my husband gets back then,' Mary Ellen would say reassuringly to someone distressed over some minor trouble. 'He is at the Judge's Javelin. They wouldn't send him back for this. . .'

It would have been hard to get any of the happy constables back from the fleshpots of Dolgellau. Most of them would drink more than they did at any other time in a year. Many of them would sicken themselves with ale—and lose their false teeth on the way home! P.C. Williams himself had been known to lose both upper and lower set and, with head throbbing and suffering from an acute sense of humiliation, search for the missing dentures in the grey light of morning, knowing that he could hardly hope to communicate with people without them.

The village always seemed quieter upon his return. He found it pleasant to come back, to hear the cocks crowing, and even to smell the pigs in the pigsties of the village. He considered his own river better than Dolgellau's wider and more spectacular water. He looked for fish more hopefully, knowing that when it had been raining a long train of salmon would move up from pool to pool, stocking each one temporarily until the next heavy downpour. He could tell just by looking at the level which pool would have a fish in it and, if it had gone up, where it would be resting.

It was when he was on duty one Sunday morning immediately following a spell at the assizes that P.C. Williams spotted two salmon, isolated in a very shallow pool, under a bridge just beyond the village. He was waiting for his sergeant who was due to come along and rendezvous with him to discuss steps to be taken about sheep scab offences. While he waited he saw how easy it would be to simply walk down to the water's edge and pull out a fine fish of perhaps nine or ten pounds without as much as getting a foot wet.

Sergeant Morgan when he arrived, agreed with him.

'It looks like rain, Williams, I think,' he said.

P.C. Williams didn't disagree. The rain was rather far off, but the sergeant's remark prompted him to put on his cape. The sergeant did likewise.

'Now Williams,' said the sergeant, 'I'll stand up here and you go down there and haul them out, teh?'

The worthy sergeant wasn't going to be caught in the act, it seemed, but he was prepared to keep lookout and that was fair enough. It took P.C. Williams less than five minutes to haul out the two salmon and knock them on the head with his truncheon. The truncheon was a rather handsome piece of equipment bearing royal arms and initials. It had rarely been put to better use. It proved just the thing for quelling a salmon, for it had quelled many a belligerent drunk. Wearing their capes, constable and sergeant tucked their fish into their respective right armpits and walked in company down the road, the sergeant proving himself extraordinarily adept at hiding his fish and at the same time wheeling a bicycle. The deed was done, and at least two police families would eat well in the following week! God was in his heaven. The world was at peace, the church bell was chiming, although on this particular occasion P.C. Williams was prevented from attending by most pressing business. He and the sergeant headed for the police station, putting on as good a step as their respective burdens would permit. All might have gone well but for the arrival of their inspector, who alighted from his bicycle behind them and bade them both good morning. If the inspector had been a stickler for salutes, and the sergeant and constable had been foolish enough to comply, there would surely have been some explaining to do when the salmon dropped to the ground, but the inspector ignored their lack of respect.

He fell in beside them.

'Well,' he said, 'since we are all here, and it's expected that we show ourselves at church, that's what we'll do. On parade, yes? The vicar will be glad to see three of us at the back!'

There was nothing to be said. The sergeant and constable did their best to renew a slipping hold on the salmon their capes concealed and followed the inspector to church.

'You expecting rain, Williams?' asked the inspector.

'You never know, sir,' he replied, groaning inwardly.

'Williams is hardly ever wrong, sir,' said Sergeant Morgan.

P.C. Williams could have wished that the sergeant had taken a little of the responsibility and said that he was wearing his cape at the sergeant's suggestion.

They stood at the back of the church, each of the two salmon-snatchers praying silently not for their souls, but for the blessing of being able to hold a slippery fish for an hour without it falling onto the floor of the church.

'This place has a strange, fishy sort of smell,' said the inspector after a while.

'All old churches have this smell, sir,' said the constable. 'It's the damp, see?'

'Strange smell,' said the inspector. 'Fishy. . .'

Sergeant Morgan hunched a shoulder and appeared to be suffering from some kind of cramp. Constable Williams held on for all he was worth.

'Damp sir,' he repeated, 'and the hymn books, given out by Mary Lewis. She sells fish sometimes. . .'

'If she does she surely washes herself before she comes to church on Sunday?'

The whispered conversation drew the vicar's attention but he smiled at the three police officers. 'I want to talk to you today about the way Christ fed the multitude, the story of the loaves and fishes. Now there are two versions in the gospels, but it really doesn't matter how many loaves and fishes Christ distributed. . .'

P.C. Williams listened and prayed that the salmon wouldn't fall while miracles were being related—two fishes and no bread. . .

It seemed an age before the sermon came to an end. The inspector looked from one to the other of them.

'I can't think why you two men should want to stand sweltering in your capes. It doesn't seem right to wear a cape in a church. I'm not wearing a cape, am I?'

'It probably didn't look like rain to you, sir, when you set out, but it looked like rain to us,' said P.C. Williams, shuffling to the door, quite certain that at last the fish was going to slither away from him.

'You better put your cape on now, sir,' said Sergeant Morgan, 'because it's coming!'

Sure enough, the slate flags and the stones outside were being spotted with large drops of rain.

'I told you, Williams is never wrong about this kind of thing,' said the sergeant. 'Only very seldom.'

The inspector looked at the sky and sniffed again.

'You know the smell of that church seems to follow you outside. I never smelt anything like it.'

'Not the same smell out here, sir,' said P.C. Williams. 'Now it is fish you can smell. They been feeding old fish heads and that to the pigs over there!'

The inspector sniffed again and climbed on to his bicycle.

'I'll be in to see you tomorrow, Williams,' he said as he rode off. The sergeant and the constable watched him go and began to walk uneasily back to the police station.

'That was a near thing, Williams,' said Sergeant Morgan. 'I wouldn't like to go through that again.'

P.C. Williams agreed. He had been feeling his years of late, but never quite so heavily as in that hour in church.

'I'm getting a bit old for excitement, Sergeant,' he said

as they parted. 'If I have too much of it I won't live to draw the old pension.'

The constable's salmon was duly delivered to his wife, while the sergeant's was made into a respectable parcel which he could tie on to the crossbar of his bicycle.

On the following morning the inspector duly arrived to check over the Occurrence Book. He compared the list of offences with those recorded in the same month of the previous year.

'Time you nailed somebody for poaching salmon, Williams, eh?'

'Well sir,' said the constable, 'there isn't really a time. You have to have fish in the pools before you can snatch them. If the fish aren't there they can't be snatched and it isn't much use trying to catch a poacher who isn't there is it?'

The inspector raised his eyebrows. 'I do a bit of fishing myself, Williams. I know when there are fish and when there aren't any. You nail somebody! Another thing, you were telling me the smell in church was damp, the hymn books, Mary Lewis not washing, the pigs being fed old fish heads, and I don't know what! All very good theories, Williams. I got a theory myself if you'd like to hear it. You know what I think? I think the smell had something to do with two police officers wearing capes in church. Now, I can't prove that that was what it was about, but if I were you I'd get your wife to sponge your tunic. There are a few scales still sticking on your sleeve and you smell of fish something awful!'

P.C. Williams knew better than to admit anything.

'I am sure Sherlock Holmes would work it out like that, sir, but believe me, that church is damp and Mary Lewis doesn't wash any more than once a year, and you can see for yourself the pigs had fish heads in their troughs.'

He wisely said nothing about his tunic smelling of fish

or the scales which the inspector was picking off with a point of a pencil.

'I don't suppose you're having stew for dinner today, Williams,' was all the inspector said as he took his leave.

P.C. Williams watched him go and sniffed. The reek of salmon scales and slime was strong. He should have had his uniform sponged! He smiled when he thought of the inspector getting after Sergeant Morgan in due course. 'I was having a word with Twenty-one. Told him it was time he caught somebody snatching salmon! Show the squire he's on the ball. Told him a little theory of mine about the smell in the church. Said I thought it had something to do with you two wearing your capes.'

He wouldn't say more than that. A man got to be an inspector by the fact that he was a wily bird as much as anything else. It wouldn't have done to have brought it all out in the open, before the public. The inspector, if he had really known about the salmon, had punished them. If he had only come to the conclusion that the salmon were hidden under the capes when the vicar was giving his sermon, then he too, probably prayed that nothing would happen in the presence of the congregation.

'What did you say, Williams?' asked his sergeant when they met again. 'The inspector was enjoying himself. He said the smell in church was something to do with us having capes on.'

'You know me, sergeant,' said P.C. Williams, 'I say nothing to any charge. I keep my tongue between my teeth. Whatever the inspector said he couldn't prove anything. If he knew, he missed his chance. I don't think he knew when he took us to church, but he knew when we came out! He's smart all right, and he can get his own salmon when he wants one.'

It was some considerable time later that P.C. Williams found himself in difficulty because of his interest in fish and fishing. By what turned out to be an almost Providential blessing of circumstances the same inspector was involved. It happened that on his day off, and after he had made careful plans to fish, the river proved sullen and the streams that flowed down into the valley were equally reluctant to part with their trout. It was hardly the month for good fishing, for it was July, and those who go to fish for trout in July frequently bemoan the fact that the trout have lost interest. Salmon brood in the pools and sea-trout move only after a freshet or soft summer rain that stipples the pools at night without driving the midges and moths to shelter. By day trout lie behind rocks and seem to doze, and there is little that even the most skilled angler can do to make them take the artificial fly. P.C. Williams toiled manfully in all the places where he might have expected a trout to rise, seeking the shadows under over-hanging trees, the colder pools below waterfalls and the out-pouring of the lake, but all to no effect. It became obvious as the day wore on that if his reputation as a catcher of men was untarnished, his reputation for being able to catch trout when no one else could might be in jeopardy. He wandered on and on, followed by the cloud of summer flies that he gathered from the browsing cattle in the fields, and fanning himself with a frond of bracken to keep the pests at bay.

It was later afternoon before he became resigned to turning back with an empty creel. No man can be success-ful all the time. Everyone admits defeat somewhere along the line. He came from the bank of the river, along the stream, and then up on to the road at the bridge and slowly plodded homeward, his rod taken down and held in his hand. It was while he was walking along, deep in thought, that he was overtaken by a youth who asked him if he had had any luck.

'No luck, boy. The fish aren't rising anywhere today,' he replied. 'If they are, I'd like to know where!'

'I know where,' said the lad. 'I seen them on Bryn Teg

lake. They're rising there like mad. You can see them from the road.'

The policeman scratched his head. He knew about trout. It was unlikely that the Bryn Teg lake was any different from anywhere else, but at least he could look and see. When he drew level with the field in which the lake stood among trees, perhaps fifty yards from the road, he couldn't see whether the fish were rising or not. The sun was in his eyes and the surface of the lake, or as much as he could see of it, was glittering like silver beaten by a silversmith's hammer. It was only when he had straddled the fence and gone half way to the water that he began to see that the fish were boiling out of the water every so often, fine fat trout, gold and silver in colour with a sheen of green about them that made them look like some exotic ornament from an Egyptian tomb. The temptation to cast a line to the rising fish was more than the policeman could resist. In a minute or two he felt the first one take his fly and bore down into the deeps, making the rod tip vibrate and the line cut water. After that he was a lost man. The wine of the country went to his head. The late afternoon was a blinding haze of silver and gold. His heart sang as he fumbled with two, three, four and five fish, which he took off the hook and put into his creel. In an hour he would have the creel full. This was living, and he lived, forgetting that he had ever sat writing tedious reports or erasing smudges from the Occurrence Book.

It was a timeless experience that could have ended with the creel being filled or the sun going down, or the fish just ceasing to rise, but none of these things happened. Instead, a hand clamped down on his arm and he turned to find himself looking at Edwards, the Bryn Teg keeper.

'Well, Williams, I'm not riding my bloody bicycle without a light now, am I?' demanded the keeper.

'No, Edwards, you're not,' he found himself replying.

'And you're the one breaking the law, trespassing, fishing in private waters?'

He said nothing. He knew that the stupidest thing any offender could do in such circumstances was to volunteer any kind of explanation.

'Right then,' said the keeper taking out a small notebook. 'I'll have your particulars if you please.'

The policeman bit back what he had a mind to say and gave his name.

'Arthur Howell Williams,' he said, 'Police Constable Twenty-one, Merioneth Constabulary, County Police Station, Abergynolwyn, Merionethshire.'

The keeper licked his pencil and laboriously wrote down what he already knew.

'Now, Williams, we'll see what you've poached . . .' he said.

P.C. Williams tipped out the contents of his creel. The trout looked a picture as they lay on the green grass. The keeper counted them and reached for his captive's rod and creel.

'No, Edwards,' said the policeman, 'you can write down in your little book that I refused to part with the rod and the creel. Now that's the whole business. You do your job and I'll go and do mine.'

'You can be sure I'll do mine, Williams,' said the keeper. 'You'll be hearing about this afternoon's bit of poaching, I can promise you that!'

Back on the road the sun seemed to have darkened. P.C. Williams walked home deep in thought. The consequences of his folly had quickly impressed themselves on his mind. Now he was in trouble and there was no way out, no excuse. The police were supposed to uphold the law, to respect property, to assist in the prevention of offences, not commit them! Mrs Lloyd Thomas, the owner of the little estate, would surely send for the inspector. She would write to the Superintendent, if not the Chief Constable. He would be out of the Force by the end of the month.

'You realize, Williams, that you will not only be dismissed, but charges will follow?' he could hear the Superintendent saying, and in three or four years wherever he went to live people would point him out as an ex-policeman, the chap who got slung out for poaching. They were all the same, policemen, one law for them and another for the public, but once in a while they even turned against their own. . . Oh, he knew all the cruel and bitter things some people said about policemen. What troubled him more was his shame in Abergynolwyn, where the vicar treated him as a man of importance, where he guided everybody in trouble and where he was trusted and liked by almost everybody, even those he had put away for a month or two. It was worse when he thought about the rest of his family, his close relatives, the others who had been in Police service.

When he got back he went in and sat at his table, pushing aside the papers that lay there and the odd fishing fly he had been toying with before he set out.

Mary Ellen came to tell him his tea was ready.

'What's wrong?' she asked, when she saw the look of despair on his face. 'You got in some trouble, Arthur?'

'Edwards caught me fishing in Mrs Lloyd Thomas's private lake,' he said. 'I've done it this time! If he has his way I'll be charged. The least that can happen is that I'll be thrown out. She'll report it to the inspector. She may even write to the Chief. I'm for the sack. I've made a right mess of everything and all for a few trout. . .'

Mary Ellen shrugged her shoulders. 'You better let one thing come at a time. It can't all happen at once. It probably won't happen. . .'

But she knew that he was in a dangerous situation if the keeper's vindictive nature had its way.

'Come and eat your tea.'

He couldn't manage to eat and he went to bed without either his tea or his supper. He didn't sleep but thought about the family being turned out of their house and having to go looking for shelter like mice disturbed from the bottom of a rick. He sighed and tossed and turned and found no comfort anywhere. In the morning Mary Ellen forced him to eat something before he went out. He walked up the road and came back again, afraid to venture far in case the inspector arrived and wanted an explanation. The charge, if a charge was made, would be read to him, no matter how familiar he was with the regulations and caution: '. . . and I must warn you that anything you do say may be taken down and used in evidence. . .' Not 'evidence against you', 'used in evidence', like the trout and the statement made by Edwards: 'I caught Police Constable Williams fishing in Bryn Teg lake. He said nothing. I made him tip out his bag. He had seven trout of about a pound each in weight. I took down particulars but he refused to part with the rod and creel. I told him I would report him and he would be hearing about it.' How many times, standing on the other side of the fence had he himself contributed a word or two in evidence against some poor fellow who had been unable to resist the temptation to cast a fly at a rising fish?

Late that day he met the sergeant and waited for some small hint that there was trouble coming, but the sergeant said nothing. He looked at the book and checked over the record of sheep scab visits.

'The river is low,' he said as he left. 'I don't suppose you've been doing much fishing?'

In a weak voice he said that he hadn't. He dared not speak about the thing to anyone. It haunted him.

'We won't be here long, I'm afraid,' he said to Mary Ellen. 'When it comes it'll fall like a mortar shell. Mrs Lloyd Thomas listens to everything Edwards tells her. He is the boss there. He'll see to it!'

Mary Ellen hurried back to clear up the dinner things. She didn't want to hear any more of it either. She couldn't live under this kind of threat and she wished he would go and make a clean breast of it all before the Superintendent sent for him. He had thought about that, but some small thing that niggled at the back of his mind cautioned him to wait. It wasn't a gambler's hope for he wasn't that sort of man. It was a peculiar sort of half-obscure vision of things not quite as they had at first seemed destined to be. There was no relief in it, and yet he had a feeling that when he had suffered long enough things would resolve themselves and the sun would begin to shine.

The sun didn't shine that day or the next but, if anything, the sky darkened on the third day, for the inspector arrived. He came bundling into the office and sat down, taking a sheaf of papers and thumbing through them without really looking at them.

'What's up, Williams?' he asked.

'Nothing sir, nothing,' he said.

'Sergeant said you seemed to have something on your mind. Now what is it, Williams?'

'I told you, sir, nothing.'

'Nothing then! I think you're a bit of a liar, Williams, but if you say you're not worrying I can't contradict you.'

They went outside after a while and walked down to the river. The pools were even lower than the day before and the stones looked bleached, and dry as lime round a kiln.

'Not the weather for fishing, is it?' asked the inspector dropping a small stone into the pool.

He noticed the outline of a fish which had been painstakingly cut on a stone of the parapet.

'Somebody either caught a big one, or wanted somebody else to think he had,' he remarked.

'Caught a big one, sir,' he said. 'It was me. I laid it there and traced round it. You wouldn't catch much in

that pool today, but believe me that wasn't a tiddler. It
was exactly the size you see on the stone.'

He said this without a lift in his voice. His gloom was
so apparent that the inspector returned to the subject.

'Look Williams,' he said, 'you've served under me for
a long time. I know you well. What's the trouble? Tell
me, and maybe I'll be able to help you.'

'Nobody can help me, sir. I'm going to get the sack.
Maybe she hasn't sent for you, but she will. Edwards
will see to that.'

'She? Who? What are you on about?'

'Mrs Lloyd Thomas, Edwards her keeper, Bryn Teg!'

'She has sent for me, Williams. Last Wednesday.
What's it got to do with you?'

'I was caught by Edwards, fishing in the private
lake. . .'

The inspector was grinning at him. 'You're a right
pessimist, Williams! You were caught by Edwards. I was
caught by Edwards! Mrs Lloyd Thomas sent for me.
All right. What about it? I said I was very sorry. She
wasn't too bad at all. She gave me permission. This is
where the buck stops, Williams. Edwards won't get past
me. I said when I was up there that one or two of my
men are keen fishermen and maybe she might give them
a chance. She said she would. You ask me you won't
hear another thing. You can rely on me anyway. If she
sends for me again I'll talk you out of it. Don't worry
any more about it. The Super won't be told.'

P.C. Williams looked at the inspector and his voice
was quite hoarse.

'Thank you very much, sir,' he said. 'I could hear you
reading the charge over to me . . .'

'When Edwards caught me there was a minute or two
when I could hear an inspector from Dolgellau, or the
Super himself, cautioning me before he read the charge,
but I soon got over that. Edwards didn't like it, but he

had to lump it and I expect she'll have told him by now.'

Mary Ellen could tell just by looking at the expression on her husband's face that things had improved.

'Well,' she said, 'we're not being thrown out?'

'I'll be here until the end of my time, I hope,' he told her. 'I'm not the only one gets caught for poaching. The inspector was nabbed too, but of course, he is a wily bird and he got round it. I could hardly be done without his being done as well, could I? Nobody will be charged. You know the old inspector isn't such a bad fellow. I've met a damn sight worse!'

12

The End of the Road

PERSONAL DIARY:
I retired from Merioneth Constabulary today. Sorry to go. I have had a very happy time here.

RETIREMENT often occupies the thoughts of a policeman more than it does those of other men. P.C. Williams plodded on without being moved to another station. He knew his place so well that he seemed to own it, and yet, as the family grew and went their own way, he knew that the day was fast approaching when he would come out of the Force and become what he hadn't been since the age of eighteen, an ordinary civilian, a villager no different from any other. It was true that at St David's Church he was organist and vicar's warden, and he was integrated in the community through his work for the St John Ambulance Brigade, the Legion, the Fishing Club, but putting off his constable's tunic and hanging up the helmet was only part of retirement. He would have to move house and he would have to find work to supplement the fifteen pounds a month which the Police Pension Fund would provide.

'The time is coming,' he told his wife, 'and coming fast, with Kenneth growing up and the others gone. I've got to think about it.'

And he went off and thought about it while he fished the river. He thought about it when the lesson was being read. He even thought about it when the letter of complaint reached him via the Chief Constable's Office, although this time there were no gloomy thoughts of being sacked from the Force. Indeed it was the only complaint ever made against him, and he had his leg pulled about it, for it concerned the appointment of a lay-reader.

It is a rule that a complaint against a police officer is conveyed to him by his superiors to give him an opportunity to answer any allegation the public may have made. The Chief Constable must have smiled when he received the letter condemning P.C. Williams, for the motive for the allegation was not concealed: 'P.C. Williams is unfit to be Vicar's Warden at St David's,' said the writer of the letter. 'He has appointed his relative as lay-reader when there is another person who should have been chosen and is better fitted to be the lay-reader. He spends too much of his time on church work and such things. Anytime you can see bikes without lights being ridden through Abergynolwyn and cars parked without lights. This should be looked into!'

The letter was copied and the copy sent to P.C. Williams requesting his attention to the matter.

'You see this?' Arthur asked his wife, brandishing the letter. 'You know what it says? Not fit to be vicar's warden—bikes without lights!'

'Is it signed?' asked Mary Ellen.

'Signed? Well it is, and it isn't!'

He took a pen and altered the typewritten signature.

'Now it's signed the way it should have been signed!'

The signature read Hugh ap Shite. Ap in Welsh has the same meaning as Mac in Gaelic—son of.

Later in the day the sergeant came and told him he was looking into allegations that P.C. Williams was spending too much of his time on public affairs, getting his relatives promoted into high positions, and discriminating against good citizens such as a certain Hugh ap Evans! Would it not be better to go out and catch a few people riding bikes without lights, even although in summer it was hardly dark before midnight and the roads were deserted?

P.C. Williams looked sourly at his sergeant. 'You ever hear him speak? You imagine he could be heard halfway down the church? I got a good mind to look out for him and book him for something. It wouldn't be hard, I can tell you!'

But he wasn't a man to bear a grudge and he almost forgot about it except that he filed the letter amongst his personal papers.

When, at last, he made his final entry in the Occurrence Book, his furniture and effects were moved down the Dyssyni Valley to a cottage he and Mrs Williams rented in the village of Llanegryn. The vicar of St David's shook his hand when he left. The villagers watched him go with some anxiety for the future. He had been more than a decade in the place. His ways were known to them, as theirs were to him. There was a danger that a newcomer might prove less understanding and more difficult to get along with than a constable who had been so long in charge.

He made his farewells one by one.

'Watch it,' he told the worst of the poachers. 'Don't think the new chap won't be on your neck. He's got to make a show, and he will! All at once he'll be out, booking you right and left. He won't be like me, happy to spend all his days here. He'll have you, so try to keep out of trouble.'

People shook his hand and were sincerely sorry to see him depart. At that moment they recognized him as the scourge of the wrong-doers, the man who had chased them, fought them, rapped their backs with a stick, pleaded with them and cajoled them.

'He was a good man, old Williams,' they said. 'A sod sometimes, but fair play, he had his job to do! He booked you, but he warned you first. He helped your mother or your wife if you were put inside. He spoke for you when you asked for a job afterwards. Fair play to him. The new bloke will never be half the man he was.'

When all the handshaking was over he found himself a villager in Llanegryn trying to be that and no more, and finding that the world still somehow saw him in a helmet and tunic. Indeed it wasn't long before the vicar at St Mary's, the parish church, was gently suggesting that, if he cared to allow his name to be put up, he might be elected People's Warden. In due course this came about. He played the organ and served as People's Warden and found employment as bailiff on the River Dyssyni. The salmon came in October, as eagerly as ever and were caught in the feeder streams for miles around by all sorts of men, women and children whether they had rods and licences or waded in to grab a fish. He caught his share of fish and poachers.

The happy life of ex-Police Constable Williams might have continued in this fashion but fate had decided otherwise. He had barely retired in 1940 when the phoney war ended. In a short time he was pressed into service to help with the Local Defence Volunteers. He became commandant of the local detachment of the Home Guard, and tried to remember his 1914-18 army training without recalling the horrors of artillery barrages. In the meantime the police authority thumbed through records and discovered his. Soon he was out of the business of drilling a platoon and sworn in under the Defence Regulations as a War Department constable, soon promoted, as he had never been during his peacetime police service. He held the rank of detective-sergeant and worked in and

about a Royal Ordnance factory near Wrexham. It wasn't
the same as being a policeman in Abergynolwyn. There
was nothing quite like being a village policeman, nor were
the people he encountered anything like the villagers of
places in the Dyssyni Valley, but sharp, crafty, near-
criminal characters who had no intention of changing
their way of life.

'I hate it,' he told his wife when he came home. 'They
steal everything and anything—money from their mates'
pockets, petrol from cars, clothing coupons, food! They
don't steal because they're poor, or have eight or nine
children. They steal because they were born to it! Give
me an honest poacher or a gipsy any day! It's like the
workhouse crowd. I fill my pocket book with their statements and their lies. They go on stealing while good lads
are getting killed. They make me sick. I wish it was
all over!'

But it wasn't over quite as quickly as his war had been,
if it was less bloody. He plodded on round the factory
and its car parks by day and by night. This world was
blacker than the woods in which he had chased poachers
and much more grim than any of the places in which he
had kept vigils for chicken thieves. There was no Occurrence Book to be kept up, but he had to prepare evidence
for presentation in court when one of his cases resulted
in a prosecution. A return to Llanegryn was like a holiday
in some wonderful place about which it seemed he had
only dreamed.

His youngest son was destined to go into the Welsh
Guards and Detective-Sergeant Williams and his wife
both fervently hoped that by the time he went the war
would be over and the war was over before young Kenneth
was old enough to join up. When at last Arthur Williams
returned to Llanegryn, Mary Ellen managed on his
pension, for he was no longer able to work. It delighted
him to learn that in a short time Guardsman Williams

had become Trained Soldier Williams, and then, at eighteen, the youngest sergeant ever in the Prince of Wales's Battalion in which he had signed on as a regular.

The First World War had taken toll of the soldiers, sailors and airmen who fought in it from its onset. It continued to claim its victims even when some of those who died in the Second World War were beginning to be forgotten. Ex-P.C. Williams suffered continually from a disordered heart, the result of shell-shock and bronchitis contracted in the trenches. In 1962 the ex-village policeman died. They remembered him in Abergynolwyn, in Trawsfynydd, in Penrhyndeudraeth, Ffestiniog and Blaenau. He was recalled by tramps, beggars, farmers, poachers, chicken-thieves and rogues, for he had been his 'brother's keeper', the representative of law and order in these places. He hadn't risen to Chief Constable, Superintendent, or even sergeant, a rank which both his brother and father had attained without much effort. His path had been a little different from theirs. He was buried at Festubert and dug up again to be invalided home and he had been posted at last to the quietest of quiet little villages in the Dyssyni Valley. He had served out his time, being what he had loved being, a village policeman and a character in his own community.

When a policeman dies, even after he retires from the Force, former colleagues, men who served with him, will always be among the mourners. The funeral of the man who was every policeman's village policeman was exceptional. It was attended not only by a great many ex-village policemen. The Lord Lieutenant was present, together with the Assistant Chief Constable.

P.C. Williams was buried in the churchyard at St Michael's, Llanfihangel-y-Pennant, among some of the old poachers he had so often chased in the woods and along the roads of the Dyssyni Valley. Six policemen carried his coffin from the church to the grave, one of them his youngest son, who had by this time left the Guards and joined the Gwynedd Constabulary. This Force had taken in the whole of Merioneth, where the old Merioneth Constabulary was now defunct.

'He was a good man,' said the vicar, 'a gentle man, and one who was highly thought of in the community in which he served.'

The ghosts of the old poachers surely nodded as the policemen filed past and saluted.